Traci,

Thank,
This book is a little different from the
last, but I hope you enjoy it.

Distorted Perception

This is a work of fiction. Names, characters, places, and incidents either are the product of the author's imagination or are used fictitiously. Any resemblance to actual persons, living or dead, events, or locales is entirely coincidental.

Copyright © 2022 by Trish Arrowsmith

All rights reserved. No part of this book may be reproduced or used in any manner without written permission of the copyright owner except for the use of quotations in a book review. For more information, address: trisharrowsmithauthor@gmail.com

First paperback edition February 2022

Book cover design by Nirkri@fiverr

ISBN 978-1-7367559-4-5 (paperback)
ISBN 978-1-7367559-5-2 (ebook)

www.trisharrowsmithauthor.com

For my sisters.

I'm convinced I stole the love of the written word from both of them, yet they've consistently been two of my biggest supporters throughout my writing journey.

I love you guys!

Preface

When I got the idea for this book, it was simply that, an idea. I didn't know where it would go, how it would end, or what I wanted it to mean. As I got further along in the writing and planning process, I realized it wasn't meant to be a *fluffy, flowery* piece. It didn't have room for vivid descriptions or side stories.

It is written in a straightforward, matter of fact way, designed to show the thought processes of an individual who finds themselves in an unpredictable, and often, dangerous situation.

It showcases how easy it can be to fall under the spell of a manipulative individual and how our heart often has more control over our actions than our brain.

Chapter I

The house rumbled from the force of Maxwell slamming the door. "Kathleen. Where are you?"

His voice penetrated the air in the hall and Kathleen froze.

"Get out here." The tone in his voice is the one she had come to fear most; the deep roar that told her he was not willing to entertain anything other than direct answers.

"Stay here," she whispered to her two youngest children. "Coming." She tried to keep her voice light and cheerful, but the word caught in her throat, betraying her. Her heart was pounding. She could hear the rush of blood in her ears. She walked the length of the hallway with her head down and almost ran straight into him when he stepped in front of her. Startled, she took a step back and struggled to find the willpower to look him in the eye. He towered over her, she could sense his anger radiating from his body.

"Is there anything you'd like to share with me about the past few days?"

He was so close the heat of his breath spread across her face. She took another step backward toward the kitchen and he matched it, closing any distance she tried to put between them. "I...I don't think so."

"Are you sure about that? There's nothing you want to tell me about, I don't know, maybe the conversation you had with Allison while she was here?"

She continued her retreat, with Maxwell matching her every step, until she felt the pain of her lower back slamming into the edge of the counter. He leaned into her; a cold sweat broke out over her body. She could feel her nerves getting the better of her as she began to shake. "She just came by to say 'hi.' You know I'm the only one who still speaks to her."

"Wrong answer."

She flinched at the sharpness in his voice.

"What did she tell you while she was here?"

She knew she had to be honest with him. "She told me the truth: about you, about this place, everything." With the last word, she swung her arm wide and knocked a juice glass to the floor. She jumped from the sound of it crashing against the wood and Maxwell seized the opportunity to pin her to the counter.

"Well. You do know how to be honest." His look of anger dissipated; a vicious smile crept across his face. His voice was calm and even. "Now, you do understand I can't have two of you running around here knowing the truth. I can't take that kind of risk." He raised his eyebrows and cocked his head. "So, it looks like I have a decision to make." He released the grip he had on her and turned away. "Or maybe," he stilled before turning his head to look deep into her eyes, "I'll let you make the decision for me."

Kathleen winced. She shook her head from side to side and her vision blurred as her eyes teared up. "I don't...I can't...please?"

"What do you think, Kathleen?" He reached out and ran his fingers down a lock of hair that was framing her face; a gesture she used to see as a sign of affection. "Who's it going to be? You? Or her?"

Tears spilled over and rolled down her face, she couldn't speak. She knew her choice would sentence one of them to death.

Thirteen Years Earlier

Chapter II

The crack of the bat snapped her out of her daze. The crowd cheered and a thunderous noise reverberated from the metal bleachers beside her. "Run, Chris, go." Kathleen found herself caught up in the excitement and joined in the applause. This was the first home game of the season and Kathleen had always believed an important part of being a teacher was showing support for her students both in and out of the classroom.

"Wow. He did really good." Vicki practically yelled in her ear, trying to be heard over the roar of the other spectators.

"Well, Vicki, he did well. You're a freakin' teacher for Christ's sake." Kathleen chuckled as she corrected her best friend's verbiage.

"Whatever. The point is that was a good hit and I'm glad you made me come with you. I didn't think I would have this much fun."

As she spoke, a gust of wind blew her hair in her face and Kathleen wondered how she could see anything. Always being the more practical of the two,

Kathleen had changed out of her work clothes and now donned a pair of sneakers and jeans. She had traded in her blouse for a sweatshirt showcasing the school's mascot and pulled her dark, chestnut hair into a ponytail.

Vicki was still wearing what she wore to school that day. Choosing looks over warmth and comfort, she watched the game in moderately high heels, a black skirt of questionable length, and a short-sleeved shirt with a silk scarf tied around her neck. It was still chilly in the evenings and Kathleen could see bumps forming on Vicki's arms.

"Hey," she whispered to Kathleen with a nudge from her elbow. "Do you see that guy over there? He's looking you up and down and he is cuuuute."

Kathleen looked across the field to find the man she was referring to. Vicki wasn't wrong. The man was attractive, at least as far as she could tell from such a distance, and it was obvious they were not the only two who thought so.

"Oh, you mean the one that has three other women hanging off him?" Kathleen rolled her eyes. "Yeah, I see him." While she sized him up, he turned his head and looked directly at her. He acknowledged her with a quick nod of his head and turned to address the other women. Kathleen took advantage of the moment and pulled her eyes away from him. She tried to concentrate on the game again but fought the urge to look at him.

Vicki swatted Kathleen's arm with the back of her hand. "I think he's coming over to talk to you. Ooh, he gets cuter as he gets closer. If you don't like him, you better introduce me."

Kathleen glanced at her sideways. "You're ridiculous. And I highly doubt with all those women over there that he's coming over here to sweep me off my feet." She couldn't help but follow him with her eyes as he walked around the perimeter of the fence. She wondered if he really was coming over to talk to her. "Besides, he has a kid with him, look."

"So what? You're around kids every day. What does it matter if it's at school or at home? He's cute, you're single, make it happen." Vicki looked at her with a sideways grin on her face. "And I'll leave you to it." She turned on the ball of her foot and walked away.

Kathleen did her best to return her focus to the game, but she could feel him getting closer and it made her uncomfortable. Knowing that he was staring straight at her, she became aware of how she stood and the expression on her face. She started to fidget with her sweatshirt and her face twitched from trying to find a casual, natural look.

"That your kid out there that hit the triple?" He asked nodding toward the field.

He was a few years older than Kathleen had first thought. His brown hair was peppered with gray strands that shimmered in the fading sunlight. He had laugh lines around his mouth which Kathleen took as a good sign. His build was strong, it was clear to her that he took care of himself. His pants were pressed, his starched collar was evident above his sweater's neckline, and his shoes had a shine to them like he had just taken them out of the box.

"Uh, no. I don't have any children. I teach at the school so I like to show my support by coming to watch the games when I can." She shyly looked at the ground and noticed that she was digging the toe of her sneaker into the dirt. It was a nervous habit that she'd had since she was small. She forced herself to stop. His shoes were spit-shined, and she was purposely scuffing hers up. She was sure it was a great first impression.

"Uh, do you have a child playing?" As soon as the words left her mouth, she knew they sounded dumb. She couldn't think of any other reason he would be here unless he was a teacher, like her, from the visiting school.

"Actually, no, I don't. This is my nephew, Cayden." He pointed toward the boy that seemed to be hiding behind his leg. "I brought him to the game so he can decide if he might want to play next year." He tried to push the child forward to acknowledge Kathleen, but he wouldn't budge. "I'm Maxwell, by the way," he said as he extended his hand.

"Kathleen." She reached out to shake his hand. "Nice to meet you. And nice to meet you, as well, Cayden." She turned back to the game unsure of what else to say. She glanced to her left and she could see Vicki standing at the end of the bleachers giving her a thumbs up with a goofy grin on her face. Kathleen closed her eyes and turned away. She had to fight the urge not to laugh.

"I hope you don't mind my coming over to talk to you. I saw you from across the way and, well...you caught my eye."

"I did, huh? With all these other women around, I was the one to catch your eye?" She smirked at him so he knew she wasn't trying to sound uninterested. "Judging by the way you're dressed you don't seem like the type to be overly impressed by a woman in a pair of jeans and a sweatshirt." Thankful for the teasing tone in her voice, Kathleen still wanted to kick herself.

"I'm not."

"Oh." Kathleen felt her heart drop. Maybe she had interpreted his words incorrectly. Heat flooded her cheeks. She hoped the embarrassment she felt hadn't caused them to grow pink.

"I'm impressed with a woman who's practical. It's cold out here and you seem to be the only one who has noticed. All these other women have to be freezing."

Kathleen smiled and nodded with relief. She had been thinking the same thing only a few moments before he walked over.

"So, this may seem a bit forward, but do you think I could convince you to go out to get a coffee with me sometime?" He stared straight at her as if he already knew she would say "yes".

Kathleen had to admit that she was intrigued by his confidence but also somewhat irritated by his lack of concern for her relationship status. "How do you know I'm not married?" She was surprised by her own reaction. She was never that forward but there was something about this man, Maxwell, that seemed to give her a boost of confidence.

"I don't. But one can hope." He flashed her a sheepish smile. "So, what do you say?"

Kathleen thought about it for a moment longer. She scrunched up her face and replied, "I'm not sure. We just met."

"And that's the point of going out, so we can get to know each other a little better. I'll tell you what. I'll give you my card with my cell number on it. If you decide you want to take me up on my offer, give me a call."

Kathleen reached out her hand, took the extended card, and folded it in her palm. "Thank you. I'll think about it."

Maxwell gave her a once over and nodded. He turned to leave but paused and looked back at her. "You can tell your friend she can come back now."

He had a mischievous look on his face that made Kathleen want to strip her clothes off and attack him right on the bleachers, in front of everyone. Thankfully for her, he put his hand on his nephew's shoulder and walked away.

Before she could react, Vicki ran up and jumped on her. "What happened? What did he say? Are you going out with him? Tell me everything, hurry up." She bounced up and down. Her excitement over the whole thing was exhausting.

All Kathleen could do was shake her head until she was sure Vicki was done asking questions. "Yes, he asked me out. No, I don't know if I'm going. I don't even know him." She flipped his business card around in her hand. Before she realized what she was doing, Vicki snatched it from her.

"What's this? Oh my god! Katie, he's a lawyer. Did you know that? Now you have to go out with him, you don't have a choice. A lawyer, Katie!"

"You know that doesn't mean anything to me. But it does make me question why I'm friends with you. And besides, being a lawyer only guarantees that he's good at one thing. Lying." She smiled at Vicki and ripped the card from her hand, putting it in her back pocket. "I told him I will think about going out with him and I will. Probably."

Kathleen laid on her couch and stared at the ceiling of her bungalow style home. It was a modest, two bedroom, right on the outskirts of the city. Kathleen was proud of it. The one thing she wanted from a young age was a stable place she could call home and she worked hard to make that a reality.

Growing up, she had little support from either of her parents and they moved around often. Every time she got comfortable in a new place and a new school, they packed up their belongings and moved again. Her dream was to find a steady job and a permanent home. She put herself through college using scholarships and worked part time so she could afford to buy herself a car. Kathleen earned her degree in education and was able to pay off her car within the first year of having a full-time teaching position. After that, her focus shifted to finding her forever home. Less than two years ago, at the age of twenty-four, she was able to make her dream a reality. She loved her house and had put a lot of time and energy into painting and decorating it to make it truly feel like her own.

The only thing she felt was missing from her life was someone to spend it with. Most of her days and some nights were spent around her students and their families. As much as she loved it, she longed for a family to call her own. She wanted someone to come home to.

She sat up on the couch and flipped Maxwell's business card back and forth. She wanted desperately to call him but was afraid to look too eager. As usual, she had doubts because it seemed too good to be true. Dating was the one place in her life she lacked confidence. Why would a lawyer, a good looking one at that, be attracted to her when he had all those other women around and obviously interested in him? Still, she knew she would be upset if she didn't follow through to see what might come of it. Even if it didn't work out, she felt she should at least try.

She had just met him the day before but had spent all the previous evening and the better part of her day thinking about him. She loved that he brought his nephew out to see the game. She kept replaying their conversation in her head and was taken by his charm and confidence. She was daydreaming about what going out in public with him would be like. She had already taken the time to look up his law firm on the internet and from what she could tell, it was a legitimate practice. Money didn't mean much to her, but she had to assume being a lawyer meant he was a hard worker and she thought, if nothing else, she may get a nice dinner or two. Before she could talk herself out of it, she picked up her phone and called him.

They spoke for almost an hour and the conversation went better than she expected. The two made plans to meet that coming Saturday for coffee and a light lunch. When she hung up the phone, Kathleen immediately sent Vicki a text to tell her she had taken the leap and called Maxwell. She felt obligated to tell her best friend, but she was also so excited she wanted to yell it from her rooftop.

While she had hoped for a quiet evening at home, Vicki forced her way over to Kathleen's house. Despite her protests, which she knew were fruitless, Vicki greeted her as she slid past her on the way to her closet and began to tear it apart. Kathleen tried to remind her that Maxwell didn't seem to care what she was wearing but Vicki was having none of it.

She knew Vicki was looking for what she would consider 'date attire' but Kathleen didn't own clothing like that. She had casual clothes and work clothes. Her work clothes were mostly dress pants and button up blouses. Her casual clothes were jeans and sweaters for winter and shorts and t-shirts for summer. She wasn't overly thrilled with her body type like Vicki was, so she stuck to what she knew worked. She couldn't even be adventurous with color choices. With her light brown hair and blue eyes, she should be able to wear anything, but her skin was pale. She always found bright colors washed her out and made her look sickly, so her closet was lined with purples, maroons, and olive greens.

Not leaving her with much of a choice, Vicki decided on an outfit for her while Kathleen sat slumped on her bed with her hands folded in her lap like a child. Her date clothing consisted of a pair of black dress pants, and a purple, satin, button-up blouse with short sleeves. It wasn't the sexiest outfit for a first date, but it did meet Kathleen's need to be practical. It also helped that she always felt comfortable and confident when she wore that shirt.

The morning of their date, Kathleen shook with nerves. It had been months since she had been on a date and the last few had been nothing short of disastrous. She had high hopes for this one but wasn't sure what to expect. Maxwell seemed so sure of himself and put together and Kathleen had days when she needed to double-check to make sure her own shoes matched. She had been anxious for days, worried whether she would do everything right. She tried to keep an open mind and hoped that, at the very least, he would like what he saw enough to ask her out a second time. She took her time dressing, applied a minimal amount of make-up, but still found herself with over an hour to spare before she had to leave to meet him. She busied herself by doing a bit of light housework, but her mind kept wandering off to what she might expect from their date. She wanted to go into it with a positive mindset, but she was psyching herself out.

The day was warm, the spring sun was shining. Aside from being nervous, she was also excited and wanted to run all the way there to meet him. When she entered the café, she saw that he had already chosen a table for them. It was exactly what she would have picked. It sat in the far, front corner with windows on two sides. Sunlight flooded the table and they would both be afforded a view of the early tree blossoms. They made eye contact and Kathleen waved at him with just her fingertips. Maxwell stood to greet her as she approached the table.

"You look lovely." He cupped her arm with his hand and leaned forward to kiss her on the cheek. She wasn't used to men treating her so properly and it wasn't the kind of introduction she expected. She thought it would be much more casual than he made it appear. She managed to get a good look at him before they both sat down. He wore the same type of outfit he had on the day they met. He had traded in his green sweater from their first meeting for one of a muted lilac and instead of a white collared shirt, today's was a plum purple. She wondered if he had any casual clothing or if he was all business, all the time.

"Thank you." She gave him half a smile and flushed with the knowledge that her nerves showed on her face.

"I'm really glad you called. I didn't think to take your number before I left." He grinned at her and winked. "Not that you would have given it to me anyway."

Kathleen laughed and immediately felt more at ease. The waitress walked over and placed two glasses of water on the table. Both Kathleen and Maxwell ordered iced tea, a sandwich, and a bowl of soup. They joked about ordering the same items yet wanting opposites of each other: one sweetened tea, one unsweetened, one ham sandwich and one turkey, and one bowl of French onion soup and one minestrone. It was a good icebreaker and freed them from the awkward silence a first date usually faced at the beginning. They conversed while they ate their lunch and ordered coffee and a slice of cake for dessert. Two hours passed in what seemed to Kathleen to be about twenty minutes. Maxwell was easy to talk to and she felt like he listened to her and cared about what she had to say. He was a far cry from the last few men she had dated.

As soon as she got home, she picked up her phone to tell Vicki about the date. "It was amazing. It may have been the best date I've ever been on. He was a perfect gentleman the whole time. He was upfront and honest about what he was looking for and he went as far as to say that he didn't want to waste my time or his...right before he asked me for a second date."

"So, what did he say he wants? I'm assuming if he asked you for a second date, he doesn't just want a quick roll in the hay. That part is a little disappointing but also promising."

Kathleen chuckled. Typical Vicki, always using sex as her go to for everything. She had to take a deep breath before she could explain what it was that Maxwell was looking for. "Well, he wants a wife. He wants children. He hopes for a stay-at-home mom for his future children because he would prefer to have them home schooled. It's just so perfect for the type of life that I've always wanted. I mean, don't get me wrong, I love my job, but you know I've always wanted to have the opportunity to stay home and teach my own kids from there.

"I'm still in awe over the whole thing. It's almost like he's been reading my mind for most of my life. He's everything that I have always said I wanted in a man. It makes me a little hesitant if I'm being honest. I mean, of course I want it to work out, but I feel like maybe I'm getting too excited too fast. Like, I'm so happy after just one date that something is bound to go wrong. You know what I mean?"

Vicki sighed and Kathleen knew she fully understood. Vicki always seemed to have the worst luck when it came to dating. Every time she called Kathleen and told her she had a great time, it was a guarantee that she would never hear back from the man again. She rarely left a first date with the promise of a second, but when she did get one, the date usually got cancelled. Kathleen assumed it was because Vicki either came on too strong or appeared too desperate. She kept her fingers crossed that she would have better luck than Vicki usually did.

The second date they had scheduled was for dinner at a fancier restaurant than she was used to. Kathleen had never been to this restaurant before and had to look it up to see what the dress code was. She chose a flowy, flowery dress, black with miniature beige and pink flowers, that fell just above her knees. It was one that she would normally have picked for parent-teacher conferences or a ceremony for the end of the school year so she figured it would be fancy enough for dinner. Like the first date, she was ready much earlier than she needed to be. Her nerves weren't acting up nearly as much this time, so she sat on her couch with a book to pass the time before he arrived. Maxwell had offered to pick her up and she accepted, thinking it would be nice to have a ride if she chose to have a glass of wine or two with dinner.

    A loud rumble outside pulled Kathleen out of her reading trance. When she looked out her living room window, she saw an old, rusty truck, in desperate need of a bath, pulling in. She wondered who it was in her driveway. The only person she expected was Maxwell. Trying to shield herself behind the curtain and the wall, she watched intently to see if it was him who emerged. To her surprise, it was. She laughed a little at the way she crouched beside the window and then let out a sigh. She had expected him to show up in a brand-new Mustang or maybe a Porsche. Even a truck was fine, but this was not a new, sleek, flashy vehicle. She thought, if she sat on the seat, she may fall through the rusted-out bottom. She plastered on a smile and opened her front door to greet him.

Like last time, he greeted her by laying a gentle kiss on her cheek. He lingered just a bit longer this time. He walked her over to his truck and opened the passenger side door for her. She was impressed by his manners. It wasn't often she found a man that was still willing to make these gestures.

Kathleen thanked him and tried to climb into the truck but noticed a box sitting on her seat. It was silver and tied with a yellow bow. She turned and looked at Maxwell with a quizzical expression on her face.

"It's a gift. For you." He grinned and gestured to the box. Kathleen didn't know what to say. She took the square box off the seat and pulled at the ends of the ribbon. She was shocked to see, when she removed the top, that it contained a little black dress.

Seeing the look on her face Maxwell replied "I thought every woman loved this kind of dress. It's supposed to be a staple or something, isn't it?"

"Uh, yes. Yes, and it's very sweet. I just didn't expect something like this." While she spoke, she set the box back on the seat so she could pull the dress fully out of the packaging. "I mean, it's only our..."

"It's only our second date. I know. But I told you, I'm not looking to waste either of our time. I asked you out again because I really like you, Kathleen. I think we may have something here between us. If I'm wrong, I apologize." He looked genuinely hurt and Kathleen felt her heart drop into her stomach.

"No, I love the dress. And yes, I agree, we may have something. I'm just not used to being treated like this. And it's moving fast." She sighed heavily. "It's nothing against you, it just... it almost feels too good to be true, you know?"

He nodded at her. "Hop in. Let's go get some dinner."

When they got to the restaurant, Kathleen was surprised. It was a quaint Italian place that only had about ten tables inside, all of which only had two chairs. It was candlelit and had a romantic ambiance. The waiter came over immediately after the host had seated them, greeted them in Italian, and poured two glasses of red wine without them ordering it. Kathleen looked puzzled and Maxwell chuckled. "I hope you don't mind. I ordered it when I made the reservation."

"I don't mind at all. But now I'm certainly glad that you're driving." She smiled and lifted her glass.

Maxwell raised his own glass and moved it her direction. "I'd like to make a toast, to us, and the hopefulness that I feel for our future." The glasses clinked together; they both took a sip.

It was the best wine Kathleen had ever had. She had to stop herself from gulping it down and asking for a second glass.

"If it's okay with you, I'd also like to order our meals?"

"Uh, sure, yes. It's Italian food, after all. I don't think it's possible for anything to be bad." When he asked if he could order she never imagined that he would order in Italian. Kathleen was both impressed and relieved since she noticed, when she picked up the menu, the entire thing was written in Italian. She was used to places that had pictures on the menu and she would have been embarrassed having to inform Maxwell that she had no idea what any of these words meant.

While they waited on their food, Maxwell asked her questions about her job and her goals for the future. He brought up their previous conversations from their phone exchanges throughout the week and inquired as to whether she would give thought to leaving her job to home school her own children. She didn't hesitate to answer him that, yes, she would absolutely quit her job for that. Kathleen loved her job, she loved the children, but as motivated as she was to own her own house and have a stable career and income, more than anything, she wanted the chance to raise her own children. She knew she could provide a supportive, loving home for her children, unlike how she was raised. She loved to bake and cook for others; she had the credentials to teach. Being able to homeschool her children would be a dream come true. Maxwell seemed to be more than pleased with her answers and equally delighted that she answered with no hesitation.

They chatted a bit more over dinner and Kathleen could feel herself slowly falling in love with him. She was afraid if he asked her to marry him today that she would say yes without even thinking it through.

When they pulled into her driveway, Maxwell shut off the engine and walked her to her door. When he asked her if he could see her inside, she politely declined. Kathleen wanted to allow him in more than anything, but she was also afraid of how it would make her look if she was to be that vulnerable so soon. To prove to him that it was nothing personal, she boldly asked him for a third date; he was quick to accept. As she unlocked and opened her front door, Maxwell slipped his arm around her waist and spun her back to him. He leaned in and met her lips before she had any time to protest. She felt her entire body want to collapse under his touch and she wanted so much to tell him she had changed her mind and lead him inside. Instead, she stood her ground and simply smiled and told him "Good night."

Chapter III

The following morning Kathleen couldn't wait to tell Vicki about her dinner date. She didn't have to wait long since Vicki practically ran to her car as she pulled into the parking lot at school. She hopped in the passenger seat before Kathleen could even fully stop her vehicle. Kathleen couldn't help but laugh at the intensity on Vicki's face. "I guess you'd like details?" She looked at the way Vicki was crammed in her car. Her legs were much too long for her to be able to fit comfortably. Kathleen was still driving her first car; the one she had in college. She'd thought about buying a new one since it was almost twelve years old but there was nothing wrong with it yet. She also didn't want the burden of having a car payment on top of a mortgage payment.

"Um, yeah, of course I want details. Tell me everything." She was like a puppy waiting at the door for its owner to come home from work.

Her eyes were wide with anticipation. Kathleen half-expected her to start panting and bouncing up and down. She took in her outfit of choice for the day. Her eyes were immediately drawn to the "V" in Vicki's sweater that showed too much cleavage to be considered appropriate for work. The heels on her knee-high boots made Kathleen's feet hurt just thinking about walking in them and she was sure the pattern of her skirt was just drawn on her skin with a marker. She didn't know how she was able to get away with this every day or, better yet, why she would want to. Kathleen certainly wasn't prude, but she did have some sense of modesty.

She scrunched up her face while she told Vicki about the gift she had received and immediately moved on to tell her about the conversations they had and their first good night kiss. She made sure to mention up front that she did not invite Maxwell in. "I just didn't want to give in too quickly in case he judges people on stuff like that. I really like him, Vicki."

"Well, I'm extremely disappointed that you didn't sleep with him, but the rest is exciting. What did you tell him about the dress?"

"I thanked him for it and told him it was sweet. The last thing I wanted to do was insult him by telling him that it is not my style. At all. I mean, it's so short. And tight. When I tried it on last night, I thought I was going to bust out of it like a warmed can of biscuits if I took a breath.

The only thing good about it is I won't have to worry about ever getting hot if I wear it. Seriously, I'm pretty sure a hand towel has more fabric than this thing."

Vicki snorted at the last comments. Of course, she would. She could wear dresses like that and be perfectly comfortable while Kathleen thought of them more as bedroom attire. The two parted ways when they entered the main lobby of the school. Before they got too far apart Vicki spun around and yelled down the hall to Kathleen. "Let me know how your next date goes, Biscuits."

Kathleen curled her lip and glared at her. "That's not funny," she retorted and chuckled to herself as she made her way down the hallway.

Kathleen waited hours hoping to hear from Maxwell. Just as she stepped out of her classroom to head to lunch, she felt her phone vibrate in her pocket and her heartbeat quickened. She unlocked her phone while she locked her classroom door.

Good afternoon, Beautiful! Hope you're having a great day. Can I call you later? ~M

She had to put her phone away to stop from texting him back right away. She felt like a teenager again. She was so happy to hear from him that she had to promise herself she wouldn't send him a reply until she was on her way back from lunch. Her level of discipline only went so far. She kept her own promise but figured she had read his message about 300 times before her break was over. When she did finally get back to him, she kept her message simple.

Hi. Sure!

When she got home, she poured herself a glass of wine, graded a few papers, and sat on the couch waiting for his call. When her phone finally rang the conversation was much shorter than she had hoped it would be. Maxwell apologized but told her he was unexpectedly stuck at the office. They did finalize their plans for a third date and Kathleen was thrilled about getting to see him again. The downside was that Maxwell asked her to wear the dress he bought for her. Without thinking, she promised him she would and while she spoke her inner voice screamed at her for promising such a thing. Why didn't she just tell him the truth? She had no idea how she would pull off wearing a dress like that. She would have to wear it all evening and she had wanted to rip it off two minutes after she tried it on. She thought maybe that was his whole plan all along. The thought both excited her and made her uncomfortable.

As promised, on the day of their date, she put the dress on to make him happy. She could barely stand to look at herself in the mirror. Unlike Vicki, who was tall, thin, and curvy in the right places, Kathleen was barely five and a half feet and she had no curves to speak of. She liked to consider herself lucky that she had shiny hair and a pretty face. She paced around her bedroom for a few minutes trying to think of a way to get out of wearing the dress. She heard his truck rumble into the driveway. She swore and ran into her closet, grabbed the only pair of kitten heels she owned, and pulled out a lightweight cardigan that fell just above her knees. On her way down the stairs, she slipped the cardigan over her shoulders, but it didn't offer her any type of relief.

It wasn't until they were inside the restaurant that she finally got a good look at Maxwell. He was immaculately dressed, as always, and it made her even more uncomfortable. He wore an argyle sweater in green and brown and dark brown pants. She was glad to see that he at least owned pants in a color other than black. She wondered if brown pants were considered casual for him. As they made their way through the restaurant, Kathleen pulled her sweater tightly around her. She felt out of place and could feel the other patrons' eyes on her.

Maxwell had chosen an Irish American pub for dinner. It was another place that Kathleen had never been before although she loved Irish food. She had already made up her mind that she would order a corned beef and Swiss sandwich and her stomach grumbled with anticipation. She was overjoyed when Maxwell ordered the same thing as her and she had to take a moment to think about how sad that was on her part.

Throughout dinner, Maxwell told her about his family and his upbringing. The only family member he had left was his sister, who he was quite close to, as far as Kathleen could tell. She did her best to listen and absorb what he said while she fussed with her dress. While he told her of his parents' demise, she tried to grab the fabric to pull it away from her stomach. It was so tight it felt like a wet bathing suit that clung to her with all the strength it could muster. Her eyes darted around the room while she checked to make sure no other diners could hear the suctioning noise she convinced herself it was making. "When I was fourteen, my brother was in a fatal car accident. He had just turned sixteen. I don't think I ever quite got over his passing." Kathleen lifted her butt off the seat and wiggled as she tried to pull the hemline lower on her thighs. Maxwell cocked his head and gave her a look that screamed annoyance. "Are you okay?"

Kathleen stopped fidgeting and looked at him while she bit her bottom lip. She sighed, "Oh, Maxwell. I'm so sorry. I promise, I was listening to you but...can I be honest with you about something?"

He looked confused. "Of course you can be honest. I wouldn't expect anything but honesty."

She closed her eyes and before she could lose her courage, blurted out, "I hate this dress." She waited a moment before continuing, thinking that Maxwell may be mad or upset, but he looked like he was ready to burst out laughing. "I'm sorry. I love that you were thinking of me when you picked it out, but it makes me very uncomfortable." She leaned forward and whispered, "I feel like I'm naked."

At the last comment he finally let go and let out a hearty laugh. "Oh, Kathleen. You should have told me. I didn't know it would make you so uncomfortable. But I am happy to see that you improvised by wearing the sweater." He chuckled again and she couldn't help but join him.

"Well, I didn't wear it for that reason. It's always cold in restaurants."

Jokingly, Maxwell replied, "Mhmm. Come on, liar. Let's get out of here. I'll take you home so you can get out of that thing." He gave her a sideways glance and raised his eyebrows. "I could probably help you if you think you need it."

Kathleen blushed and was thankful that be that the restaurant was dimly lit so Maxwell couldn't tell. She giggled a bit to make it seem like she thought he was joking when every part of her screamed, "Yes, please."

At two in the morning, she casually grabbed her phone and leaned over the side of her bed, hoping the light from the screen wouldn't wake Maxwell, and texted Vicki.

It was magical!!

By date number five, Kathleen had fallen in what people refer to as "head over heels in love" with Maxwell. She knew at that point she would be able to spend the rest of her life with him. He was kind, thoughtful, and sociable. He had an air about him that made everyone love him. At first, she thought it was his looks and confidence that attracted women to him but as time went on, she found that men were drawn to him as well. Every person, regardless of gender or age found it necessary to engage him in conversation. It made her feel special to know that she was the one he chose to spend his time with. She had never needed the type of confidence that came with dating a certain type of man, but now that she had it, she was more than happy to walk around with a bit of eye candy by her side.

One of the things she liked best about Maxwell was that he listened to what she had to say. A few weeks after the dress fiasco he showed up at her house with no prior arrangements and had another gift for her. She squinted her eyes when she opened it because it came in the same box as the last gift. This one was adorned with a pink bow rather than yellow. She was pleasantly surprised when she opened it. It was another dress, but this one was one hundred percent her style. It buttoned down the front, was a knee-length "A" line, and had the smallest, sparsely placed feather print on it. The deep maroon color didn't hurt either. It was perfect. She dropped the box on her couch and gave him the biggest bear hug her strength would allow. "I love it. Thank you so much."

Maxwell pushed her to his arm's length, looked her in the eye, and smiled. "I'm glad you love it...because I love you."

Kathleen almost dropped to the floor. His words took away her ability to speak for a few moments while she gathered her thoughts. After her heart rate returned to normal, she squeaked out "I love you, too." She could feel tears of happiness stinging her eyes and she did her best to fight it.

Maxwell smiled. "I really do hope those are happy tears because I don't know how to take those words back."

Kathleen laughed and melted into his embrace. "I really do love you."

She didn't hear from him for three days after that visit and started to get worried that those three little words were the end of their relationship. She had said it before, numerous times, that she thought it was too good to be true and she began to believe she was right. She had allowed herself to be vulnerable and that was a turn off for him. She showed him her heart and he was going to break it. She'd had it happen before and she didn't think she would be able to mentally handle going through that process again. It was too hard to go through and too hard to try to start over with someone else. At times, she wasn't sure it was worth all the pain and aggravation. After trying three and four times a day, she had made up her mind that she would not text him again. If he wanted to see and talk to her, he would have to be the one to make that move.

Maxwell waited another two days before he contacted her. Kathleen had been struggling with her emotions, hating him one minute and missing him the next. She wanted so badly to ignore him or give him attitude for ignoring her, but she didn't have it in her. She missed him too much to play games with him. He apologized for his absence and explained that work had pulled him away from life for a few days. It was a short conversation, but Kathleen was thrilled to hear from him. They made plans to meet for coffee that weekend once Maxwell got back into town. As expected, the reunion after little more than a week was like heaven for her. When Maxwell stepped onto her porch, he embraced her, picked her up from the ground, and spun her around like they were teenagers. Kathleen squealed with delight as she realized he missed her as much as she missed him.

By the time they got to the coffee shop, Kathleen thought she could feel a bit of tension between them. She tried her best to shrug it off but because their reunion felt so loving only a short while ago, she broke down and asked him if something was bothering him.

Maxwell shook his head and his eyes met the table. "No, nothing is wrong. I just feel bad that I didn't give you any warning as to what work can be like sometimes. When I'm working on a big case, I have to put all my effort into my work and I tend to lose all connections with my personal life. I didn't mean to do that to you. You didn't deserve to have me disappear like that. My sister is used to it, and since I don't really have anyone else in my life that would notice, I kind of forgot that you hadn't experienced it yet. If I'm to be honest, I was really worried when I noticed I hadn't heard from you in a few days." He let out a nervous laugh. "I guess I have no room to complain there. But, I thought that maybe you had given up on me. On us." He sounded sincere and it almost made Kathleen feel bad for him, even after what he had put her through.

Kathleen gave him a look of sympathy. "To be honest, I didn't think I had a choice. I sent you a few messages and when I didn't get a response, I just assumed your silence was your response. I thought you had made the decision to move on." Maxwell reached over and gripped her hand in his. "I wasn't quite ready to accept that but decided to leave it up to you if you wanted to contact me again." She shrugged her shoulders and cocked her head in a nonchalant "I don't know" type of gesture.

Maxwell looked devastated. "Just please know, in the future, I don't ever mean to disappear like that. But my practice means a lot to me. I really need to try to plan better around my personal life but it's easy to get caught up when it's a big case. There is always a lot riding on cases like these for both me and the firm. And I really like my job, I don't want to risk losing it. I've worked really hard to get where I am."

"I understand. I just hope that in the future, since you seem to be planning one with me, you'll send me a quick message to let me know that you'll need to be away for a while. At least that way I won't feel the need to question myself, or us."

"That's a fair request." Maxwell promised that he would do his best to make her feel like she's a priority in his life, because she is.

After coffee, he asked her to join him for a stroll on the boardwalk since it was such a beautiful day. The air was warm, the sun was shining bright. At the start of the walk, Maxwell took her hand in his and held it gently. The sun glistened off the water and they could smell the aromas coming from the few food vendors that decided to open their trucks early for the season. Even though they had just had dessert, it made them both hungry. As they made their way further down the boardwalk, Kathleen began to feel the same tension from earlier. Maxwell's hand began to sweat, and it started to feel like a clamp on Kathleen's own. She tried to ignore it but when Maxwell released his grip she gave in again. She stopped walking and turned to face him. "Is something wrong?"

He had a look of distress on his face. "No, not at all." He took a deep breath, exhaled, and grabbed both of her hands. "Kathleen, I love you. At this point in my life, and hopefully in yours as well, I am ready to settle down. I know it may seem fast, but I don't ever want to let you go. You mean the world to me and I want the whole world to know it." He let go of her hands and dug around in his pocket before he dropped to one knee. He looked deep into her eyes as he opened the small box containing a diamond ring. "Will you do me the honor of becoming my wife?"

Kathleen almost passed out. She had to step back so she wouldn't fall over when she felt her body begin to waver. Her heart rate sped up and she had to question for a moment whether she was dreaming. "It's, well, it, um...yes, Maxwell. Yes, I'll be your wife." Her eyes immediately welled up with happy tears. It was quick but it didn't matter. She knew weeks ago that she wanted to spend the rest of her life with him. She had never been so in love with anyone before. He slipped the ring on her finger and pulled her into his embrace. She couldn't help but laugh through the tears. "You were nervous."

"Of course, I was nervous. I don't know what I would have done if you said 'no'."

Chapter IV

Kathleen was so excited when she got home, she couldn't bring herself to share the news with anyone yet. She wanted to enjoy being the only one who knew she would soon be Mrs. Maxwell Lewis. Fortunately, there were only two people on her list to share the news with. Her mother and Vicki. She couldn't decide whether she wanted to call her mother to share the news and invite her to the wedding or if she wanted to call her to gloat that she found a good, caring man who was devoted only to her. As almost every woman wants, there was a part of her that wanted her mother to be there at her wedding, to share her special day. But Kathleen also had a much stronger part of her that just wanted to rub it in her mother's face that she was going to have a healthy, loving marriage.

Kathleen was raised in a household by two parents who were extremely selfish. Neither of them had time for her nor for each other. On the rare occasion they were both home, all they did was argue until one of them got mad enough to storm out. From the time she was barely old enough to understand, they made no secret of her father's infidelities and often, her mother told Kathleen it was her fault. Being a bit naïve, as she was, Kathleen took it to heart and believed it to be true until the time she got to college. It wasn't until she moved away from home that she realized how complicated her home life had been. Less than a year after she left, her father walked out of her and her mother's lives for good. She hasn't spoken to him since.

    She laid on her couch where the sun shined through the window and turned her hand back and forth to see the reflection bounce off the diamonds. She didn't get a good look at the ring until they were on their way back to her house. It was beautiful and she figured it must have cost Maxwell a fortune. It felt heavy on her hand. She was afraid, because it stood out so far from her finger, she would hit it on everything. She would have to be extra careful until she got used to wearing it.

    Kathleen decided to call Vicki rather than waiting to see her in person. Even though she still wanted to keep the news to herself she felt like she was about to explode from excitement. Her hope was that she would be able to tell her the news but not show her the ring until they met at school on Monday. She sent Vicki a text message asking her to call. When her phone rang, she didn't even get a chance to say "hello". She could hear Vicki screaming in the mouthpiece asking her if she was okay. Kathleen had forgotten the last time they spoke they discussed how Maxwell had stopped calling her. Vicki was worried they had broken up and Kathleen was in need of a shoulder to cry on. She waited until Vicki stopped to catch her breath and interrupted her before she had a chance to continue.

"Vicki, stop. Calm down. We did not break up." She tried her hardest but couldn't stop herself from laughing. Although she could hear Vicki's annoyance through the phone, it made her happy that her best friend was so willing to have her back in what she thought was a difficult time. "I'm sorry. Your first reaction was funny to me, but I do appreciate your concern. What I need to tell you though," she paused for dramatic effect, "is that it is the complete opposite of what you thought it was." She pulled her phone away just enough so if Vicki caught on to what she was saying, she wouldn't go deaf in one ear.

"The opposite? What's the opposite of breaking up?" Kathleen tried to stay silent but she had never been good with keeping secrets. Just as she opened her mouth to respond Vicki blurted out "Oh my god! You killed him! You'll need clean up help. I can come over..."

Kathleen burst out laughing. "Vicki. No. The opposite in a good way."

Vicki was silent for a moment before it finally hit her. "He proposed?" She screamed into the phone.

Kathleen didn't have a chance to pull the phone away before the piercing screech came through on her end. "He did." She grinned from ear to ear.

"Did he give you a ring?"

"Of course he gave me a ring." Before she could say anything else, she heard Vicki slam her front door and after a moment, she heard her car start.

"Where are you going?"

"I'm driving to your place to see the ring. You can't keep this from me. I'm pretty pissed that I have to drive all the way over there. You should have been here banging on my door."

Kathleen sighed internally. She should have known that would happen. "Okay. I'll be here." She used the ten minutes she had before Vicki arrived to admire her ring alone. She knew it was weird and possibly selfish but she wanted to enjoy that part of the secret just a little longer.

Kathleen had always dreamed of a big wedding. She wanted the fluffy dress, the bountiful bouquets, and the horse drawn carriage. It didn't matter much to her that she didn't have a large family or a big circle of friends. She didn't care that she wasn't close to her mother. She wanted to invite everyone she knew. Even though she couldn't afford it herself, she wanted as many frills as she could get. She had actively thought that if she presented it to Maxwell in such a way that she could show how much it would mean to her, he might offer to pay for it.

She mentioned her idea to Vicki and the two began to plan how she should introduce the idea to Maxwell. She didn't want to put him into debt, especially since she assumed they would share a bank account soon enough, but she had dreamed of her wedding since she was a young child. Vicki was proud of Kathleen for thinking of this herself. Kathleen had told her many times that she was too quick to use others to get what she wanted. Now that the tables were turned, Kathleen understood where Vicki came from. She justified her thoughts by telling herself it was her wedding day, a once in a lifetime opportunity.

Two weeks went by before Kathleen got up the nerve to tell Maxwell what she wanted for their wedding. She truly believed that he would be more than willing to give her what she wanted to make her happy. His reaction, or lack thereof, immediately upset her. He didn't seem to care one way or the other about what she wanted. For the first time since they had started dating, he didn't seem to be listening to anything she had to say. His attentiveness was one of the traits she had fallen in love with. But now it seemed to Kathleen that he didn't have any interest in talking about the wedding, planning any of it, or hearing about what she wanted. He looked like his mind was miles away. Every now and again he nodded or threw in an "uh-huh". Tears manifested in Kathleen's eyes and she could feel herself about to break down when he finally responded to her with a real answer.

"Honey, look. I am so excited to marry you. Much more than you probably realize. But the actual planning of a wedding is just not something that men get excited about." He walked over to her and took her hands in his. To Kathleen, his touch said "loving" but his words said "jerk". "I'm willing to do whatever it is that you want for that day but I have to be honest and tell you that I really don't care, at all, about planning it." Seeing the look on Kathleen's face he paused and took a deep breath. "I just want you to be happy. Why don't you ask Vicki to help you plan everything?"

"Because, Maxwell," she ripped her hands out of his and turned her back on him, "I'm not marrying Vicki. I'm marrying you." She turned to face him again and leaned against the kitchen counter with her arms crossed. "I know that you may not be as interested in planning it as I am, but I really would appreciate some help and input. Whether it means that much to you or not, it means a lot to me. That alone should make you want to help me." She threw her arms out to the side and began to pace the floor. "I mean, you keep telling me that you want me to be happy but that's not what your actions are saying right now. Right now, all you're telling me is that you don't care. If you truly want me to be happy, you'll help me with this. Even something as simple as a yes or no to a few of my questions would be better than what you're giving me right now."

"Fine. Yes."

Kathleen sighed in frustration. "Yes? Yes what?"

"Yes. If you want it, the answer is yes. Now that I've helped, I'm going to bed."

Kathleen showed up on Vicki's doorstep in tears. She couldn't understand why Maxwell seemed so excited about marrying her but wanted nothing to do with planning the wedding. She understood that men didn't get as excited about that particular day as women did but she still thought that he should have some sort of interest in it. If she told him that she wanted to get married in the lion's cage at the zoo he should care enough to step in and say "no, absolutely not. Big cats will eat you."

Once Vicki got her to stop crying, she poured them each a glass of wine so they could enjoy a good drink while they tried to figure out how to fix this problem.

"I know I'm probably more upset than I should be, but this is our first fight. And what a thing to fight about. This is supposed to be one of the happiest times of my life and he doesn't seem to care at all."

"I think you have every right to be upset about this. He's not a teenager, he knows how important a wedding is to a woman."

Kathleen nodded. "But it's not just that. He wasn't even listening to me. He always listens. He even pays attention. Remember when he bought me that insanely tight dress? As soon as I told him it wasn't for me, he went out and got me one that was exactly my style. He genuinely seems to care about my opinions. So why is he so withdrawn about this?"

While the two of them talked, Vicki quietly planned her own solution. She made up her mind to call Maxwell herself to try and explain how much this meant to Kathleen. She believed if he heard it from someone other than Kathleen, he might begin to take it more seriously. He needed to understand that he was hurting her by not wanting anything to do with the wedding. She wanted to make two things clear to him. The first was that he didn't have to ask Kathleen to marry him. If he wasn't interested in a wedding, he should have just kept dating her. The second was that he was the one who told her that he didn't want to waste any time. He told her he was looking for a wife. He was honest about what he wanted and now he didn't want anything to do with it. What he was doing to Kathleen wasn't right and Vicki had every intention of telling him that.

Vicki waited until a day that she knew he was supposed to be at work. Rather than calling him and giving him a chance to hang up on her, she decided to pay a visit to his office. It was the worst decision she could have made. When she approached the desk and requested to speak to Maxwell, she was informed that he wasn't there and hadn't been for quite some time. Apparently, he had forgotten to mention to Kathleen that he was on a leave of absence and had basically lied to her throughout the duration of their relationship. On her way back to the car she tried to come up with some scenarios where it would make sense for Maxwell to lie. Kathleen was already upset about the wedding and Vicki didn't want to make it worse. She wanted to give him the benefit of the doubt but didn't have any luck coming up with an explanation. Where was he really when he told Kathleen that work was taking him away for days at a time? If he was on a leave of absence, what did he fill his days doing? Vicki was so angry with Maxwell she wanted to scream. She sat in her car for five minutes trying to calm herself down before having to go break the news to Kathleen. She was not looking forward to the conversation.

    Kathleen refused to accept what Vicki was telling her. She would not believe that Maxwell was not working when he said he was. Thankfully, Vicki had expected this kind of reaction and she was prepared for it. She had warned herself not to get upset knowing that Kathleen would all but accuse her of lying and being jealous enough to try to get her to call off the wedding. She knew she would feel the exact same way if she was in Kathleen's position. She could only hope that Kathleen would decide for herself to do some investigating to find out where Maxwell was.

Whether through a bit of sleuthing or simply asking Maxwell for an explanation and following up on his answer, Vicki only wanted Kathleen to know the truth. She wanted to know the truth herself. Maybe he did have a good reason for not saying anything. Perhaps he took a side job, a case that paid well that was Pro Bono. Maybe he was working for a different firm and wasn't quite ready to quit his old one yet. She doubted both of those scenarios but for Kathleen's sake she hoped he had a good answer.

Kathleen didn't know how to react. She was angry and taking it out on Vicki. She knew it wasn't fair but she didn't want to believe that Maxwell had been lying to her. She could tell by the look on Vicki's face that she was upset with her and she didn't blame her. She'd be upset if Vicki had accused her of lying. Kathleen would have to take some time to sit down and think about the conversation that she had had with Maxwell when he apologized for disappearing. Did he say that he was working for the firm? Did he say anything that should have made her question where he was? Was she so totally head over heels in love that she was too blind to see what was right in her face? It certainly wouldn't be the first time that had happened to her. She had been told numerous times throughout her life that she was nothing if not naïve and she had to agree with that. She always had a tendency to see the best in people and she knew she was easy to take advantage of because of it. She asked Vicki to leave so she could have some time to think about what was happening. She just wanted to be alone.

Vicki pushed back a bit but did as was requested. She only hoped that Kathleen would come to her senses soon. Vicki could understand how devastating news like this could be and she couldn't imagine that she would feel any different about it. She wanted to be there for Kathleen and not be pushed away when she knew her best friend needed her. She drove home trying to think of ways that she would be able to help Kathleen once she came around. She didn't want to go behind her back again but the only thing she could come up with was to try to set him up and that wouldn't be a good thing for anyone involved. She nixed the idea completely.

Kathleen curled up in her bed and cried until she could no longer produce any more tears. Her head ached and her eyes burned. She tried to get her head straight and the first thing she did was chastise herself for getting so upset when she didn't have any kind of evidence for what Vicki told her. She decided to ask Maxwell straight out where he was and who he really worked for. It was fine if he was on a leave of absence of sorts from his firm but she would like to know what it was that he was doing or at least who he worked for. She did not think it was unfair of her, at this point in their relationship, to ask him to be honest with her.

Maybe it was a simple explanation. Perhaps he was looking to change firms and he was testing the waters of a new place before he left his current practice. That would be a smart move and seemed like the type of thing he might do. Maxwell, like Kathleen, was of the practical sorts and she didn't believe that he would up and leave a firm that he had been at for years without having a solid backup plan. She just needed to work up the courage to ask him and hope that he understood where she was coming from. She wouldn't accuse him of lying or try to blame him for anything. She would simply explain that Vicki went looking to speak to him and found out, consequently, that he was not currently at the firm. It should go smoothly. She hoped.

Distorted Perception

She was wrong. To put it mildly, Maxwell was not pleased. In fact, he was livid. At Kathleen, at Vicki, and at himself for not covering better. He had to think of an excuse fast. His defense was to get mad so he could yell while he tried to figure out what he could tell her. He should have known from the beginning that he couldn't trust Vicki but at least now he knew where he had to start. Vicki would have to be removed from their relationship one way or another. He already knew she wouldn't go away easily. Vicki wasn't anywhere near as naïve or as easily manipulated as Kathleen. She was a much stronger person. Vicki was much more strong-willed than anyone else he had encountered so far and she may prove to be his biggest challenge yet.

Kathleen trembled. She had never seen Maxwell upset before and he was angry. She also never realized how deep his voice was until he raised it. It echoed through her house and she hoped that her neighbors wouldn't hear it. Her thoughts began to race when she saw how quick he was to get this mad. Fortunately, although she could see it in his body language, he chose to turn around and walk away from her. His muscles were tense, his hands were balled into fists, and his face was red from yelling. In the back of her mind, all she could picture was her father getting just as angry, except he never walked away. If Kathleen or her mother were not able to hide fast enough, they felt the full weight of his fisted hands. She wanted to lash out and scream at Maxwell to calm down or get out. At this point, either option would work for her.

Until now, she hadn't told Maxwell about her father. She simply said he wasn't part of her life and left it at that. Maxwell didn't push for more information. Kathleen hoped that she would never have to tell him specifics about her childhood. Now, if they were able to get through this episode, she would be forced to tell him so he could understand her reaction to what was happening. Her heart rate grew faster the longer she watched him in his state of rage. She began to sweat. She never would have expected this from him and she hadn't been in this situation in a long time. Memories raced through her mind as she waited for him to turn and advance on her. Tears welled in her eyes and she willed herself to keep it together. She had forgotten what it was like to feel so weak, so powerless against the simple tone of someone's voice. After this was over, she would have to tell him this couldn't happen again. This was not something she could live with. She wouldn't tolerate it.

Just when she felt as if her mind might explode, Maxwell turned to her. His general demeanor was much calmer, his face had gone back to its natural hue, and it looked like a weight had been lifted off his shoulders. His entire body seemed to relax at once. Kathleen saw the look of disapproval on his face. Not of her, but of himself. She prepared for the apology speech that she knew would shortly follow. Maxwell kneeled in front of her and reached up to caress both of her arms. He could feel her entire body shaking.

"Kathleen. I am so sorry. I don't know what just came over me. I've never done that before. Are you okay?" As much as she didn't believe him because she had been through this so many times before, he looked and sounded genuine. Even from a young age she never once believed her father when he said he was sorry. Somehow she knew, deep down, that he wasn't sorry at all.

"I'm okay, mostly. Listen, I wasn't planning on telling you this now. I don't know if I was ever planning on telling you to be honest, but I think I need to. Will you come with me for a minute, please?" Kathleen led him to the couch and when he sat down next to her his face was drawn. He looked concerned. Kathleen was still scared but her heart rate began to slow down and she knew the worst of it was over. Her voice shook but she took her time and told Maxwell about her father and continued on about her life growing up and why she's not close to her mother. She hoped that he would be able to understand why it upset her so much to see him like that. He listened to her with great intensity and let her say what she needed to say without interrupting her or asking any questions. This was the Maxwell she had grown to love.

Maxwell was awed by what she had revealed about her life and couldn't think of a response to her telling him what she went through. He stared at her for a moment longer and then leaned in and hugged her close. "I'm so sorry you had to go through that. I never would have guessed you had grown up that way." He stroked her hair like he was petting a dog. He didn't want to let her go and he didn't for a long while. They sat in each other's embrace and Kathleen could feel the love pulsing between them. Although it wasn't the best of times, she enjoyed the feeling.

She still wanted answers to their problem and she wasn't quite ready to let it go but she kept her fingers crossed that he would give her an honest response without her having to bring it up again. For now, she just wanted to enjoy the time they spent together and she wanted to continue planning the wedding. She hoped to get married in the fall and that didn't leave her with much time to plan. For tonight, she would leave everything alone. She wouldn't bring up his job and wouldn't bring up the wedding. The last thing she wanted to do was upset him again. Instead, she took his hand and led him to the bedroom.

Chapter V

Kathleen called Vicki to tell her about everything that happened the night before. Vicki couldn't seem to ask her questions fast enough. She wanted to know about Maxwell's blow up and how he reacted to Kathleen's admittance of her home life during her youth. She wanted to know what Kathleen found out about Maxwell's job and she wanted all the answers at once. Kathleen had to laugh at Vicki's sputtering through the phone. She couldn't finish answering the first question before the second one was being asked. At least now Kathleen was able to find some humor in the situation. Last night, that would have been impossible.

They made plans to meet for lunch the next day and then go shopping for new outfits. That was mostly for Vicki. Kathleen didn't enjoy shopping nearly as much as Vicki did. In truth, she loved to shop, she just hated to spend money and always ended up feeling bad about her purchases once she got home. She was an impulse shopper and bought things because they were there, not because she needed or even wanted them. She bought things because she could. Her quick purchases were worse when she was with Vicki because most times, she wasn't given the choice to say no. She practically twisted Kathleen's arm until she handed over her credit card. But what are best friends for if they can't force you to make bad decisions that you'll regret later?

Kathleen spent the rest of the day loafing on the couch. She flipped back and forth between channels but never settled on anything to watch. She couldn't seem to concentrate enough. She thought about how Maxwell blew up when she questioned him. He did not respond well at all. She had to wonder if it was because he got caught doing something wrong or if it was just because she questioned him like she didn't trust him. She did trust him. She just wanted him to be honest with her since she knew he would expect the same from her. What bothered her most was that she knew the only reason she would get mad in this situation was if she did something wrong. She didn't think she would be able to rest until she got an honest answer.

She poured herself a glass of wine and drew a hot bath to try to soak her sorrows away. It didn't help her head, but her muscles were more relaxed, and she was warm. It was only seven in the evening when she got out of the bathtub, but she put on her pajamas and climbed into bed. She thought a book would help keep her mind off her troubles.

A few days later, Vicki left late in the evening to make her daily food run. She chose the smaller grocery store since it was closer to her house. She ran through her mental shopping list as she made her way through the aisles. When she rounded the corner to retrieve a box of pasta, she stopped dead. Maxwell stood halfway down the aisle, running his hand along the small of a woman's back. That woman was not Kathleen. He nudged her with his shoulder and looked around casually until he made eye contact with Vicki. He held her gaze for a moment until recognition registered on both of their faces. He leaned into the other woman and whispered, "I have to go." She stroked the side of his face and kissed his other cheek before he disappeared around the corner.

Vicki's jaw dropped and her head fell forward. She just caught Maxwell, in public, with another woman. She wouldn't let that go. She raced down the aisle, passed the woman, and tried to find Maxwell, but he was gone. She turned back and went to confront the woman she had just seen him with. She found her two aisles down from where they had been. "Excuse me? Was that Maxwell who was just with you?" She knew it sounded like an odd question, but it was the best she could come up with.

The woman answered with as much attitude as she could muster. "I'm sorry. But who are you and why is that any of your business?"

Vicki was taken aback. She thought her question was innocent enough. "Um. I'm Vicki. It's just, the guy...the one who was just with you. He looked like someone I know is all." She hated how her voice betrayed her. Her words came out quiet and staggered.

"Well, sweetie. Seeing how quick he took off after he saw you, I would take that as a sign to move on." She cocked her head, turned on her heel, and strutted down the aisle which caused the food basket to bounce off her hip.

Vicki stood in the middle of the aisle shaking her head. "What a bitch," she mumbled. With slumped shoulders, she made her way back to her shopping cart. She couldn't believe she would have to be the one to break this news to Kathleen. Twice, within two weeks, she had caught Maxwell in a lie. She couldn't allow her best friend to marry someone who continued to lie to her.

When she got home from the store, she called Kathleen to see if she could stop over. It had been four days since they had had a proper conversation. Kathleen wasn't up for company, but Vicki told her it was too important to discuss over the phone. She put her food away and headed out. Her heart pounded; her skin was covered in a layer of sweat. When she pulled into Kathleen's driveway, she sat in her car for almost five minutes as she tried to compose herself and get her thoughts in order. She knew this would be a delicate conversation and she needed to mentally prepare for it.

She looked up and saw Kathleen standing in her doorway shrugging her shoulders. She took a deep breath. "Now or never," she thought. She walked up to the door and heard Kathleen ask, "What were you doing? I thought maybe you had fallen asleep out here." She stood to the side so Vicki could enter her house. Vicki immediately made her way into the kitchen and started a pot of coffee without saying a word. Kathleen followed her and leaned against the counter with her arms crossed over her chest. Vicki tried to ignore her, but she could feel Kathleen's eyes burning into her skin.

"Okay, okay. Stop staring at me. Let me pour the coffee and I'll come join you at the table."

Kathleen sighed and dropped her arms like a child beginning a tantrum, but she did as she was told. Vicki poured two cups of coffee and set one down in front of Kathleen before she sunk into her own chair. "Okay. So, I have to tell you something and I want you to listen to what I'm telling you before you get mad. And you need to understand the only reason I'm telling you is because I care about you. I don't want to see you get hurt." She paused, looking for some sort of reaction on Kathleen's face, she couldn't tell what she was thinking. "Anyway. I saw Maxwell tonight and he was..." She closed her eyes and took a deep breath. She didn't want to finish the sentence. She stared at Kathleen for a moment before continuing. "He was with another woman." Now she couldn't look at Kathleen's face. She stared into her coffee instead.

"What do you mean 'with another woman'? What does that mean?" Kathleen knew what she meant but wanted to know exactly what context she meant it in.

Vicki sighed. "He was with another woman. I saw him with his hand on her back. It looked pretty intimate to me. And when he turned around and saw me, he left. He didn't even acknowledge me. He just turned around and walked away." She took another deep breath and continued. "Kathleen, I'm really sorry I'm telling you all this. Anyway, I tried to talk to him, but he was gone. So, I tried to talk to the woman he was with..."

"You what?" Kathleen practically screamed. "Why would you try to talk to her? Do you know who she was?" The look on Kathleen's face was one of pure anger.

Vicki thought she would be upset but didn't expect this level of anger. "No, I don't know her. I just wanted to ask her if it was Maxwell that she was with."

"So, you don't even know for sure that it was him? Do you think maybe you should have found out for sure before you came over here and tried to accuse him of cheating on me?" Kathleen's face was bright red, her lips were drawn tight. "And not to mention, you've met him exactly twice. Briefly."

Vicki felt awful about the entire situation. "No, I do know that it was him. But I didn't want to go right up to her and ask, 'are you sleeping with Maxwell?'" She didn't know what else to say so she sat in silence.

After a moment, Kathleen stood up and grabbed her phone off the counter. "Okay, we'll do this the easy way. I'll call him and we can find out together."

"Katie."

"No, it'll be good for both of us to know. If you're right, I'll be able to cry on your shoulder. If you're wrong, you can leave my house." She hit the button to call Maxwell and put her phone on speaker.

"Katie, you don't have to do this."

"Well, apparently, I do. Because this is the second time in so many weeks that you've come to me with information..."

"Hey, Beautiful."

"Maxwell. Hi."

"Um. Everything okay?"

"Maybe. Vicki is here. She's on speaker. We're hoping maybe you can clear something up for us."

Vicki stayed seated at the table with her eyes closed. No matter what he said, it wouldn't be good news for her.

"Hi, Vicki. I'll do my best to help. What's up?"

"Vicki told me she saw you today. With another woman. Is it true?" Both Maxwell and Vicki could hear the annoyance in her voice.

Maxwell sighed audibly into the phone. "Well, I'm not one-hundred percent sure I like the way you're asking the question, but I guess honesty is best on my part."

Kathleen looked like she was about to fall over. She felt her knees grow weak and she grabbed the back of a chair for support. Vicki could see the phone shaking in her hand.

"Yes, I was with another woman. But not in the way you're both probably thinking. And I thank you, Vicki, for ruining my surprise. That other woman is my sister, Allison. I brought her out here to surprise you. I wanted you to finally meet her."

Kathleen felt like she might fall over again but this time, with relief. She looked at Vicki and pointed to the door. "Get out."

Vicki's mouth dropped open. "Katie..."

"Out," Kathleen yelled and pointed at the door again.

Vicki stood, snatched her keys off the table, and stormed out. She slammed the door as hard as she could. By the time she got to her car tears flowed down her face. How could she have been so stupid? Kathleen was her best friend and she had just delivered the worst news possible only for it to be completely untrue. She wondered if Kathleen would ever forgive her. She waited in the driveway until her vision cleared enough for her to drive. She was upset about Kathleen, but she was livid with Maxwell. None of this would have happened if he didn't run away like he did. All he had to do was introduce her to his sister and tell her that it was a surprise for Kathleen. She squealed her tires, leaving what she was sure would be an inch of rubber at the end of Kathleen's driveway.

As soon as Vicki left Kathleen started to cry. She apologized to Maxwell and assured him that she called to clear things up, not because she believed Vicki. That seemed to satisfy him, and he promised to call her in the morning. He wanted the three of them, Kathleen, Allison, and himself to get together for lunch the next day. Kathleen was thrilled that he forgave her so easily and it made her almost forget how much Vicki had upset her.

Maxwell had spent the few previous evenings pondering how to start working on getting Vicki out of the picture. A few months ago, he never would have thought she would be a problem. He saw her as completely self-absorbed and thought she would go away on her own. He was wrong about her and realized she is a much better friend to Kathleen than he thought. That wasn't good for him. He decided to start small to see if that would work for him. He called in some backup to get the ball rolling.

That afternoon, Maxwell and Allison staked themselves out in front of Vicki's house. They had stocked up on snack food and coffee, unsure of how long it would take for her to leave. They waited a little more than three hours before she emerged from her front door. When she hopped in her car, they waited for her to pass before pulling out behind her and following her down the road. She had a lead foot and apparently viewed stop signs as optional. When she pulled into the parking lot of a grocery store, they both breathed a sigh of relief. They were glad they didn't have to drive behind her anymore and being in a grocery store would make their plan as simple as possible.

They waited for her to get inside the store before they got out of the car. Their plan was very simple. All they had to do was get Vicki to see them together and then get Maxwell out of the store before she had a chance to confront him. They followed her around through half the store while Allison kept an eye on Vicki and Maxwell stayed well hidden from her view. Once they decided to make their move, they skipped an aisle ahead so they would be there when Vicki turned in. Allison watched closely and once Vicki rounded the corner, she gave Maxwell the go ahead. Vicki reacted exactly how they hoped she would, and Maxwell was pleased that his plan, so far, had worked so perfectly.

Kathleen woke the next morning with a miserable headache and a foul mood to match. It took all her energy just to get into the shower. She needed to do something to put herself in a better mood. She couldn't meet Maxwell's sister like this. Maxwell spoke so highly of her and seemed to praise her every chance he got. She hoped he spoke of her the same way when he talked to Allison. After she showered, she took a couple of aspirin and made herself a strong pot of coffee while she waited for him to call.

She was up early but still found herself checking her phone every five minutes waiting to hear from him. Hours passed by without him calling. She had washed all her dishes, swept her kitchen floor, watered her plants, and read the current news on the internet. It was after eleven when he finally called her. He told her Allison had an emergency with her son and she had to go back home. Kathleen was upset that she had missed her chance to finally meet Allison but was happy Maxwell still wanted to meet her for lunch. She wanted to see him in person so she could apologize for the phone call from the previous evening. Not knowing what he had planned, Kathleen skipped breakfast. Now her stomach growled, and she didn't think she could get to the café fast enough.

She arrived five minutes later than they were supposed to meet but Maxwell had already gotten them a table and he rose to greet her. He kissed her on the cheek. "I've missed you."

"Listen, about last night..."

"Don't worry about last night. I understand. I'm willing to forget about it if you are." He gave her a half-hearted smile that told her he was still a little peeved, but he would get over it.

She took a deep breath. "I was never mad at or upset with you. The point of me calling was to prove Vicki wrong. I was mad at her. I didn't stop to think that I might upset you, too. I wasn't thinking straight. Thank you for understanding that." She balled her hands into fists and Maxwell could see how tense her body was. "I'm still so angry with Vicki. I don't understand why she would come to me and tell me that without having any proof. It's almost like she's jealous or something. She did the exact same thing a few weeks ago, remember? That thing with your job? It's so frustrating." She banged her fists on the table.

"She's supposed to be my best friend. You would think she'd be happy for me." She shook her head in disgust.

"I get it. It's upsetting to find out that your friends may not be who you think they are. But I think maybe you just need to let this whole thing blow over and see if she comes to her senses. Maybe she just needs some time to adjust. We think everything is happening fast for us, but you have to remember that this is happening fast for her, too. You guys used to spend all of your time together and we both have to admit, I've been getting my fair share of your time recently." He pulled her hand across the table and kissed the back of it. "Just give it some time. I'm sure she'll come around."

The positivity in his words and reassuring tone in his voice made Kathleen feel better almost immediately. She was relieved that he was so accommodating to her feelings, and he was right. Maybe it affected Vicki much more than she realized. "Thank you for that. I didn't think about it that way before. And I appreciate you being so thoughtful about it. After all, you should be more upset than I am."

While they waited for the waitress to come and take their order, Kathleen took a few moments to look around. She had never been to this café before, and she adored its ambiance. The entire interior was green and white with splashes of light-colored wood. Plants hung from the ceiling and filled the floor in front of the full-length windows that went around three sides of the building. It was beautiful. Although it wasn't quite fall yet, Kathleen imagined the windows would afford a magnificent view of the foliage that announced the changes of the seasons.

Instrumental music played softly through the overhead speakers. She kept her fingers crossed that the food was as good as the atmosphere.

She was pulled from her trance when Maxwell cleared his throat and she realized he was staring at her. She looked over at him and almost burst out laughing. "Why do you have such an adoring look on your face?" She couldn't help but smile back.

"Well, mostly because I adore you. But also, because I have a proposal for you but I'm not sure how you're going to feel about it." When he said that, his look of adoration turned to one of concern. "I think, in light of everything that has happened in these past few weeks, we should get married...next week."

"Next week," Kathleen squeaked. "Maxwell, you can't plan a wedding in a week. Do you know how long...?"

He put his hand up to stop her. "I know. I know you can't plan a wedding in a week. I just think, that maybe if we got married on our own, like by the Justice of the Peace or something, it may make it easier for everyone." He raised his hand again to keep her from interrupting. "If we get married now, we can have a huge reception later. It'll give everyone a chance to get used to us being together. We can finally move in together and it'll give you the chance to plan the whole thing without us having to wait. What do you think?"

He looked pleased with himself and if nothing else, Kathleen had to admire him for that. After what she had put him through last night, he was still trying to make things easier for her. It was clear that he had thought this through. Kathleen shook her head. "I mean, it sounds like a really good idea, it's just not how I ever pictured getting married, you know?"

Chapter VI

Kathleen had no idea what to do about Maxwell's proposal. She agreed that it would make everything easier but her dream wedding was just that, a wedding. Not a dream reception. Kathleen wanted the magic of the entire day. Maxwell told her to take her time and think about what she wanted and she promised she would. He assured her she could still have everything she wanted. He only cared if she was happy.

Most of her afternoon she stared off into space and tried to decide what to do. She wanted to give him an answer as soon as she could but she felt the stress of having to make that big of a decision. Her headache returned early that evening and she thought about Vicki again. Maxwell's point about how she might feel hit home with Kathleen and that thought was what persuaded her to make her decision. She called him later that night and told him to make plans for the next weekend. In less than one week's time, she would be Mrs. Maxwell Lewis. To her own surprise, she smiled at the thought. It wasn't the wedding that would make her happy. It was him.

Having made that decision, she slept much better that night. She had to remind herself over and over that she was getting married. She couldn't believe it. Maxwell would move into her house and as excited as she was, she was nervous about having to share her personal space with someone else. It wasn't something she had ever given any thought to in the past but now she realized it would be a big adjustment for her. She didn't even own a pet that would be considered a constant companion and now she would have another person around all the time. That made her more nervous than getting married.

She considered calling Vicki to tell her what they had decided but she remembered Maxwell's words and changed her mind. She wouldn't tell anyone until after they had exchanged vows. If she waited, no one would be able to tell her it was a bad idea and no one could try to talk her out of it. She wanted so much for Vicki to be there but with how they ended their last conversation, she didn't think this news would be a good way to get them speaking again.

Kathleen spent most of her free time that week cleaning out her house. She got rid of clothes that she no longer wore and packed boxes of knick-knacks that she had collected over the years. She decided to turn the room she used for storage into an office for Maxwell. She didn't ask him if he had or needed one but she assumed it was something that would be useful for him. As she sorted through all of her belongings, trying to decide what to do with all of them, it occurred to her that there was a lot she didn't know about Maxwell. As the week wore on, she couldn't decide if she was excited, anxious, or scared about the changes coming up. She stopped numerous times throughout the week to contemplate whether this was the right choice or not.

She told herself over and over again that both men and women get cold feet when they are about to get married. She did an internet search on it to assure herself that it was a normal feeling. Even so, she still had a nagging feeling in the pit of her stomach. Numerous times the past two days she picked up her phone to call Maxwell. She hoped if she talked to him he might be able to reassure her and calm her nerves a bit. Every time she picked her phone up, she set it back down. She didn't want him to think she was having second thoughts, or worse, to hear him say that he was questioning their decision as well.

When she awoke on Saturday morning, the big day, she bolted out of bed and into the bathroom. She barely made it to the toilet before she emptied the contents of her stomach into the bowl. Sweat dripped down her face and she rested her head against the cool porcelain while she waited for her heart to stop racing. Her head pounded to the rhythm of her heartbeat. She had forgotten how much havoc her nerves could create within her body.

Once she calmed down a bit and the jittery feeling in her chest went away she made her way to the kitchen to make a pot of coffee and took a scalding hot shower while she waited for it to brew. She had no idea how long she stood under the stream of water but it felt so good on her aching muscles she never wanted to get out. When she had gone to bed the night before she was happy and she felt good. With no recollection of it she was sure she must have had one hell of a dream to wake up with her body feeling so awful. She dried herself off and wrapped herself in a robe before padding into the kitchen to enjoy her coffee and relax a bit. She wasn't expected to meet Maxwell until two in the afternoon so she made her way to the couch with her coffee and a book. It was only after eight so she had plenty of time to kill.

When she looked at the clock again it was almost twelve. She jumped off the couch and ran to her bedroom so she could start getting ready. She dug around in her closet for her dress and shoes and questioned how she could possibly have slept that long. Aside from how she felt earlier, she knew that she had gotten more than enough sleep throughout the night. She switched gears when she pulled the dress from the hang bar and admired it for a moment. Even though it was a simple ceremony with no guests joining them and no church, she still wanted to feel something of an actual wedding. She wanted to feel like a bride.

Earlier in the week she had gone out and found an embellished, cream-colored dress that fell to her knees with a scalloped edge. It had a lace overlay and she thought, for being such a simple, inexpensive dress, it was quite stunning. And it was pure luck on her part that she found it in a little hole in the wall vintage shop in the next town over. When she tried it on, she knew it needed to be hers. There was no way she could leave it there. She couldn't find a pair of shoes to match the color of the dress since it was so well-aged but she found a simple pair of satin kitten heels in a light beige that complemented the dress nicely.

She slathered lotion on her legs, put her make-up on, and curled her hair. Before getting dressed, she sat on her bed to take a minute for herself. 'Mrs. Maxwell Lewis', she thought. All the nervousness from the morning and the past week seemed to vanish. Her heart beat a little faster as she realized that in a few hours this would no longer be 'her bedroom'. It would be 'their bedroom'. Tonight, Maxwell would return home with her and he would be there to stay.

Kathleen stood and stretched. She could feel her muscles pulling against the strain. Just as she reached for her dress the doorbell chimed. She swore. This was the worst timing for someone to stop by. She poked her head around the corner and saw Vicki peeking in the window on the side of her front door. Kathleen jumped back and stood with her back and palms pressed against the wall. Her heart pounded. She hoped she moved fast enough that Vicki didn't see her.

The doorbell chimed again and Vicki rapped on the door. She peered through the window a second time. Shielding her eyes to get a better look she yelled, "Kathleen. It's me. Vicki. I know you're home. Your car is in the driveway. Anyway, I brought you a peace offering." She paused for a moment, hoping Kathleen would open the door. "I miss you. If you can hear me, call me, okay?" She retreated down the steps and Kathleen waited until she heard her car pull away before she opened the door.

It took everything she had to not race to the door and embrace Vicki and cry about how much she had missed her. If she had more time, she probably wouldn't have been able to stop herself. She peered down and saw a bouquet of daisies, tied with a blue ribbon, sitting at her feet. Daisies were her favorite. Her eyes started to well up with tears and she began to fan at them. Her makeup was already done and she didn't have the time to fix it. She walked the flowers inside and arranged them in a vase. She admired them for a moment as her table's centerpiece and ran to her bedroom to get dressed.

Kathleen pulled into the parking lot five minutes early and saw Maxwell standing outside. He was dressed in a black suit, as she had seen him many times, but he traded in his tie for a bow tie. His shoes gleamed in the afternoon sun and he had a small rose pinned to his jacket. The fact that he had thought about that made her smile. She hadn't thought about flowers for this. He greeted her at her car door and kissed her cheek when she got out.

He took a step back and admired her for a moment. "You look amazing." His smile was broad and genuine.

"Well, you look quite fetching yourself. I like your bow tie." She reached up and caressed the ends of it.

"I figured I'd get dressed up for the occasion." She could see the sparkle in his eyes and loved that he was in a joking mood. It made her feel better to see how relaxed he was. "That's a beautiful dress. Vintage?"

"I'm not sure I want to know how, or why, you know that but, yes, it is. And thank you. I found it in a tiny shop and I just couldn't leave it there."

"Well, I'm glad you didn't. It's exquisite." His eyes moved up and down the length of her body. "What do you say we go inside and get hitched?"

"Let's go." She smiled and did her best not to laugh at the phrase 'get hitched'. All she could picture was an animal being tied to a fence post.

Kathleen gasped when they entered the building. It was cold and stark. Maxwell handed her a bouquet of roses that he picked up from a small card table. It was the only bit of color in the room. Two folding chairs were displayed in the center of the room and the only wall décor was what appeared to be leftover remnants from posters and flyers of previous occupants. Maxwell introduced her to the officiant that would perform their ceremony. He stood behind a wire music stand that had one rose tied to the corner. It was already beginning to droop.

She spent the next three minutes staring at the music stand, wondering why it was there. It was empty except for the absurd attempt to decorate it. It wasn't until Maxwell leaned over and nudged her that she heard the officiant speaking to her. "I do." Her mind wandered off again and when Maxwell leaned in and kissed her, she realized the ceremony was over. The entire ordeal took less than five minutes. She glanced at Maxwell while he shook hands with the officiant. He looked pleased. Kathleen felt awful. She immediately regretted giving in to his wishes so easily. She took a deep breath and plastered on a fake grin before reaching out to shake the officiant's hand.

Maxwell handed her a stack of papers. "I signed these before you got here. You probably should have done it first, too, but you just need to sign each one to make our marriage official." Kathleen kneeled in front of one of the folding chairs and used the seat as a table. Maxwell grabbed each piece of paper from her as soon as her signature was on it.

As they walked outside, Kathleen noticed the sun hiding behind the clouds and could feel the damp, fall weather seeping into her bones. She shivered and crossed her arms over her body. Maxwell slipped an arm around her waist. "Are you okay, Mrs. Lewis?" For weeks, she had dreamed of someone calling her that. Hearing those words come out of his mouth at that moment made bile rise to her throat. This was not what she wanted at all.

She smiled half-heartedly. "I'm okay. Just a little cold."

"Well, then. Let's not waste any time. Let's go get you warmed up and we can consecrate this marriage." He had a sly look on his face which Kathleen usually found impossible to ignore. Right now, it made her stomach turn.

They had left her car in the parking lot and on the drive back to her house she wondered what was wrong with her. She had wanted to marry Maxwell from the first time she met him and she got her chance. Now she was filled with nothing but doubt. How did things change so quickly?

They spent the majority of the afternoon and evening in bed, getting up only when they decided to make dinner. Maxwell noticed the flowers on the table when he entered the kitchen. "Pretty flowers. Who'd you get those from?" His tone was polite yet quizzical.

"Um, Vicki stopped by this afternoon and left them at the door. I was getting ready to leave so I didn't open it. But she yelled in saying that she was sorry and she wants me to call her." She felt a pang of sorrow at the thought of Vicki being kept in the dark about them getting married.

Maxwell stepped over to her and wrapped his arms around her waist. "See that. I told you she would come around." He leaned in and kissed the tip of her nose.

Kathleen pulled out of his embrace. "Oh, she came around, all right. At the worst possible time. I wanted nothing more than to open the door to her but I couldn't. I didn't have time to explain anything to her and I think I owe her a proper apology. The last time she was here I told her to get out and I haven't spoken to her since. I certainly couldn't let her in today without telling her that I was running off to get married." She spat the words at him and was shocked at how angry she really was.

He stared at her, wide-eyed, unsure whether he should feel bad for her or be angry that she tried to blame him. "Do you already regret having married me? It's been, like, four hours."

The concern in his voice stamped out a lot of Kathleen's anger. She leaned against the counter and rested her face in her hands before facing him again. "No, of course I don't regret marrying you. It's just not what I ever imagined my wedding day being like. Since the day I met Vicki I always assumed that she would be standing by my side as I said my vows." She advanced towards him and rested her head on his shoulder. "I am so happy to be your wife. There's just a lot of stuff, really big changes that are all happening at once. I'll just need a little time to adjust." She hugged him to her and they stood in silence for a few minutes before breaking off to make dinner.

Maxwell didn't say another word about Vicki or about their marriage for the rest of the evening. He was too busy planning his next move.

The next day was like every other weekend they had spent together since they started dating. They both woke up early, had coffee and breakfast, and then lounged most of the day. This was one thing they had in common that they loved about each other. They agreed that one weekend day was for being lazy and anything that had to be done should either be done earlier in the week or it could wait until later on.

Kathleen was at the kitchen counter making them sandwiches for lunch when Maxwell came in and wrapped his arms around her from the back. She spun around to face him. "So, listen. I was thinking about our conversation yesterday. I think maybe you should call Vicki and see what she has to say. She's obviously willing to try to make this situation better. But I also think it might be wise to hold off on telling her about us just yet. Maybe give it a few weeks, or even a month. Let things settle down between the two of you before you break the news to her. You know she's going to be quite upset about it."

She nodded her head as he spoke. "I was actually thinking the exact same thing earlier this morning. She's going to be really upset when she finds out and I think I would rather the two of us be on full speaking terms again before I drop this bomb on her."

Maxwell winked at her and walked back to the living room. "I'll need a glass of milk with my sandwich," he called to her from the couch. Kathleen opened her mouth to respond and decided against it. Was she supposed to laugh at that? With his tone of voice she couldn't tell whether he was joking or not. She shook her head and finished the sandwiches. Luckily for him, she wanted a glass of milk, too.

The rest of the day was spent curled up on the couch, watching television. Maxwell's mind seemed to be elsewhere, Kathleen guessed it was on work. And her mind was on Vicki. She decided not to call her but planned to talk to her when she got to work the next day. It would be their first week back at school and they had meetings planned for every day that week. She couldn't bear the thought of sitting through those meetings without Vicki sitting next to her. It was still early but she couldn't wait to go to bed so she could talk to her sooner.

On Monday morning, Kathleen woke early and went to the kitchen to start a pot of coffee. Maxwell had never stayed at her house on a weeknight and she wasn't sure what to expect from his morning routine. He came in shortly after she had sat down, freshly showered, dressed, and with an overnight bag in his hand. "I have to run. I'll grab a coffee on my way." He leaned down and gave her a quick kiss. "I'll call you later." He turned and headed out the door.

'Well,' Kathleen thought, 'that wasn't quite what I expected.' She made a mental note to ask him about the bag when they spoke later. She showered and dressed quickly. She wanted to get to school early so she would have a chance to talk to Vicki before the meetings started for the day. She didn't want to wait until their lunch.

When she pulled into the parking lot she saw Vicki getting out of her car. Without even turning off her engine, she opened her door and yelled to her from across the parking lot. Vicki looked surprised but smiled and started over to her. Kathleen couldn't help but smile. She was overwhelmed with emotion at seeing Vicki's face. She waved over the roof of her car and ducked back in to collect her bag and keys.

By the time they got into the building they had already stopped to hug each other twice and each of them made fun of the other when she started to tear up. They planned to spend their break together so they could catch up on all the gossip they missed out on over the last week.

Kathleen checked her phone every chance she got waiting to hear from Maxwell. She didn't receive a message from him until she was on her way back from lunch.

Hey, Beautiful! I'm so sorry but I have to go out of town today. I should be back late tomorrow night though. Love you!

She almost threw her phone down the hallway. They had been married for less than forty-eight hours and he was already leaving. She guessed she couldn't be too angry about it. It happened before and they had never fully discussed his work schedule. Kathleen had been too afraid to bring it up again because of what happened the last time. But she was angry. She shot back a text before she could think about how she should respond.

I don't suppose you could have told me that this morning since you clearly knew you were going. You brought a bag with you.

Maxwell must have had his phone in his hand because he replied back immediately.

I bring a bag with me every day because I don't always know if I'll have to leave or not. But in the future, if you have something like that to say to me, I would suggest you don't. I'll see you tomorrow.

Kathleen threw her phone in her purse, dropped it on the floor, and slumped down in her chair. This was not how she imagined married life to be. She took her phone out again with the intention of texting Maxwell back but thought better of it when Vicki sat down next to her. She turned to her, ready to blurt out what Maxwell was doing. She needed to vent about him leaving so early in their marriage but then remembered Vicki didn't know yet. She hated hiding the truth from her but she wasn't ready to share it just yet.

The rest of the afternoon went by quickly. Kathleen stopped at the grocery store like she planned to do anyway. She bought a frozen pizza for herself and picked up a few quick items in case Maxwell was hungry when he got home the next night.

Maxwell and Kathleen had been married for almost a month. She felt much better about it now that she was used to him living with her. He had only left for work overnight a few times. She still hadn't told Vicki that they were married and it got harder by the day for her to keep the secret. Kathleen didn't feel well when she woke up that morning so she took the day off work to rest. Maxwell offered to stop at the store on the way home from work that evening to pick up dinner.

He waited for Vicki until she got out of school. He knew it was risky but he kept his fingers crossed that she would also stop at the store on her way home. He had gotten word from Kathleen that she stopped almost every day to pick up only what she needed for that night's dinner. He stayed back a few car lengths and was thankful there was a bit of traffic to slow down her driving. As he had hoped, he saw her pull into the grocery store parking lot. He had only seen Vicki once since the day she had spoken to Allison. He had apologized to her, in a half-hearted way, about running off. He told her he didn't think she had actually seen him so he left before she did. She accepted his apology but still questioned why it would have mattered if she did see him.

He followed her around the store for just a moment before they caught each other's eye. This time, he walked right up to her. He didn't want her to think he was running away again. They talked for a few minutes and parted ways.

Maxwell came barging through the door with his hands full of grocery bags. He plopped them on the counter before going to give Kathleen a kiss. "How are you feeling?"

"I still feel awful but I'm much better than I was this morning."

"Good." He started to unpack the bags. "I stopped at that little market across town today because I was over that way. I ran into Vicki." He didn't turn back to look at Kathleen he just kept emptying bags, waiting for her to say something.

"I never go over to that one. It's too expensive, I think. Did you talk to her this time?" She chuckled a little bit and half expected the phone to ring with Vicki accusing him of ignoring her or running away again. She stopped her line of thinking as she knew it wasn't fair. Vicki was supposed to be her best friend. She shouldn't be having thoughts like that about her.

"As a matter of fact, I did talk to her. I took it upon myself to greet her so she didn't think I was trying to hide something again." He turned and finally faced her. "You know, I have to give you credit. You see her every day and still haven't said anything to her about us getting married. I only talked to her for about three minutes and I wanted to blurt it out six different times. I don't know how you do it."

Kathleen couldn't help but laugh. "It's one of the hardest things I've ever had to do. I tell Vicki everything about my life. It's been that way for years. I'm going to tell her soon though. I don't think I can keep the secret much longer. It's been eating away at me for a month."

Chapter VII

The next morning, Vicki waited by Kathleen's parking spot for when she pulled in at work. It wasn't a surprise, she did it often so she could ignore all the people she didn't want to talk to. Kathleen smiled and waved. Vicki did not return the pleasantry. Before Kathleen was out of her car, Vicki yelled through her window. "I need to talk to you. As soon as school is over, we need to talk." Her body was rigid, her face pinched.

"Are you okay? Do you want to talk now, we have a few minutes before class?" Vicki shook her head. "You look like you're going to spontaneously combust." Normally, Vicki would have laughed at a comment like that. She was clearly not in the mood for joking this morning.

"No. We'll talk after school. Don't leave until I talk to you." She turned and stomped through the parking lot without waiting for Kathleen to collect her things.

Kathleen was confused. She had no idea what could have set Vicki off so early in the morning. She hadn't spoken to her since they had lunch together two days prior and she thought it could have been anything since then, maybe something that she was still steaming about because she hadn't had a chance to vent about it yet. Mid-morning, Kathleen sent her a text.

Meet for lunch?

A reply came back immediately.

AFTER SCHOOL!!

Whatever it was, Kathleen decided, couldn't be that important if she was so hell bent on waiting seven hours until the end of the school day when she could have just told her first thing this morning. She wouldn't let it ruin her day. She texted Maxwell.

Vicki is pissed. No idea why. I was planning on telling her today but…I'm not so sure now.

Maxwell called her during lunch. "Hey. What's she all pissed off about?"

"I honestly have no idea. She came storming up to me when I pulled into work this morning, barking about having to talk to me. But she's refusing to say anything until after school."

"And you didn't tell her yet? Do you think she could have found out somehow? Maybe that's why she's mad?"

She loved that he seemed so concerned about her relationship with Vicki. "No, I didn't say anything yet. Are you sure you didn't say anything to her when you saw her yesterday? Something that may have triggered the thought?"

"I promise you. I didn't say anything. We only talked for a minute."

"Okay. I guess I'll just have to wait until after work to see what her issue is. Will you be home for dinner?"

"I'll be late, but I'll be home. I love you."

Kathleen hit the end call button and scarfed down the rest of her sandwich. She'd get the answer to the mystery soon enough.

Vicki waited outside the classroom door before Kathleen even had her things packed up. She leaned against the door frame with her arms crossed over her chest, tapping her foot.

"Nothing like showing how impatient you are. You can come in, you know."

"I'm good out here."

Kathleen shook her head and rolled her eyes. She wondered what she could possibly have done since it was now obvious that Vicki was mad at her. She finished gathering her stuff, locked her desk, and met Vicki in the hallway.

"So. I don't suppose your boyfriend told you he ran into me at the store yesterday?" Her arms were still crossed and her lips were pursed even when she spoke.

"Actually, yes, he did. Why?" She narrowed her eyes, her lip curled. She could feel the coldness emanating from Vicki's body.

Vicki glanced at her sideways. "A little far from home, don't you think?"

Kathleen could feel the anger growing inside her. "He has clients all over the place. He was on that side of town for work yesterday because that's where his client happened to be. Why don't you just tell me what you want to say?" Heat crept up her neck and face and she knew her skin was flushed.

"Hmph. Work, right. I forgot. His prestigious job that he's on leave from."

"What the hell, Vicki? What is your problem?" Kathleen wasn't concerned with being nice anymore. It was obvious Vicki didn't want anything to do with Maxwell or with the two of them being together.

"My problem? I don't suppose when he told you he saw me, he also told you he hit on me?" She stopped walking and turned to Kathleen with stern indignation.

"Wow. That's what we're doing now? If you don't like him, that's fine. But why are you so insistent about trying to break us up? First, you went to his office without even asking me if it was okay. Then, you accused him of cheating on me when he was with his own sister. And now? I...I don't even know what to say anymore." She threw her hands in the air as a gesture of surrender.

"I haven't lied to you once. And this isn't about me or you. It's about him. I don't trust him and I don't want to see you get hurt. I made a mistake when I saw him with his sister. I should have asked you before I went to his office. But this time, I was there. I was part of the conversation. Your boyfriend came right out and asked me to sleep with him."

"Well, I've got good news for you then. He's not my boyfriend. He's my husband. We got married a month ago," Kathleen screamed the last few words and they echoed down the hallway. She turned on her heel and stomped down the hall and through the parking lot. Her entire body trembled, her eyes were full of tears. She couldn't believe the nerve Vicki had. And to add a little more fuel to the fire, Vicki didn't even call out after her or try to catch up with her. She just let her walk away.

As soon as she got home she poured herself a glass of wine and curled up on the couch. She texted Maxwell to tell him that Vicki knew about them and said she would fill him in on the details when he got home. How could she have been so wrong about Vicki? They had been best friends for years. She replayed the conversation they had over and over in her head. She planned how she would run the conversation with Maxwell. She didn't want him to think she was accusing him again. In her mind, this had nothing to do with Maxwell but everything to do with Vicki. She texted him again and asked him to pick up a pizza on his way home. She planned on making dinner when he got home but she was too exhausted to move off the couch.

She was jolted awake when she heard Maxwell slam the door of his truck. She must have been more tired than she thought. He arrived home later than she thought he would, but he did bring a pizza with him. He set the box on the table, got them both a bottle of water, and sat on the edge of the couch. He was all ears. Barely taking the time to say hello to him, she started right in with how everything went down with Vicki. Tears started to flow down her face. They were caused more from anger than from sadness. Maxwell listened to every word and seemed to be taking it all in. Kathleen thought he would have some sort of response after she told him everything but the words that followed surprised her.

"I hate to say it, but I think maybe you two weren't as close as you may have thought. Being jealous is one thing, but it seems to me like she doesn't accept you having a relationship at all. She should be happy that you found someone, not focused on trying to break us up." He shook his head. "It almost seems like she is the jealous girlfriend who wants all your time." He looked at her with empathy in his eyes. "Maybe you need to cut ties with her. At least for a while, until she can figure out if she really wants your friendship. Do you think you'll ever be able to trust her with anything after the way she's been acting lately?"

The last question hit Kathleen hard. She started to cry again. She didn't have to think about the answer. "No, I don't think I'll be able to trust her with anything, ever again." Maxwell leaned in and hugged her when he saw her body deflate. Kathleen melted into him and stayed there for a long time. She refused to let go of the comfort he brought her.

"Can I tell you about our friendship?"

Maxwell nodded. "Of course, you can."

"I promise, I'll try to keep it short. Vicki and I met the first day of our senior year in high school. We were both brand new to the school, so we started hanging out. We've been pretty much inseparable since then. We both wanted to be teachers. We went to the same college. Our dynamic has never changed. I've always been the responsible one that kept her out of trouble. She's always been the irresponsible one that convinced me to make some questionable decisions. I usually had a steady boyfriend and she usually had one-night stands.

"Anyway, during our junior year of college, I started dating this guy. I really liked him and we spent a lot of time together. I started going to school games and parties with him, instead of with Vicki, and she was so jealous she was actually angry. She kept telling me she was seeing him with other girls and that I needed to be careful because she didn't trust him. She told me he was being rude to her when I wasn't around. Well, I had to go home one weekend for something or another and when I got back to school, I walked into our dorm to find her, in bed, with him. Apparently, she had a crush on him before we started dating. I honestly didn't know. If I knew, I would have stayed away from him. But Vicki has always been the same. She likes a guy for a day or two and then moves on to her next victim. I happened to find the one she really liked at the time and that's how she got her revenge.

"I didn't talk to her for a few months after that and, obviously, I broke up with the guy. When Vicki and I started talking again, I told her I wouldn't allow her to act like that anymore. She needed to understand that if either of us were seeing someone, we had to give them space. Since then, she's still gotten a little bitchy sometimes if I was dating someone, but it's never been as bad as that first time. Until now."

Maxwell shrugged and raised his eyebrows. "You think she likes me?"

Kathleen laughed from deep in her chest. "Oh. I love you so much. Thank you for listening to me whine."

Maxwell pulled her into an embrace. "You weren't whining. But I'm glad you told me that. Now, I understand why you react the way you do when she tries to tell you stuff about me. It's almost like she's reverted to the past version of herself."

"Exactly."

The next few days at work felt lonely for Kathleen. She was used to seeing Vicki almost every morning and meeting her for lunch three to four times a week. She had picked up her phone numerous times to send her a message but always thought better of it. Maxwell had also sent her several messages to remind her to stand her ground. He knew how much she missed Vicki and how hard this was for her. Kathleen loved his little reminders to stay strong.

Little did she know, what Maxwell really wanted was for Vicki to be gone from their lives for good. It wouldn't do him any favors to have her sticking around. So far, she had played by his rules at every turn. He was pleased.

Chapter VIII

Two months into their marriage, Maxwell began to change. He came home one day and casually mentioned he had combined their cell phone bills. Kathleen questioned how that was possible without her permission and all Maxwell could do was laugh. "Sweetheart, I'm a lawyer. I can find out anything I want, about anyone I want. Besides, I live here now, remember? Your bill comes straight to the house. That's pretty much all I needed."

Kathleen was mad. She didn't care that he looked at her phone bill, but she thought they were supposed to be partners. All he had to do was ask her before he went ahead and did it. She tried to rationalize his behavior by reminding herself that married couples combined their bills all the time. She thought she might be too sensitive about it because she was so used to doing everything herself.

That same day, even though she was already upset with him, he sat her down and told her he wanted her to quit her teaching job. Kathleen stared at him with her eyes wide and a slack jaw. She had no idea what to say. Kathleen questioned whether he thought they should discuss, together, the idea of having children and he laughed in her face again.

"There is nothing to discuss. We're married. You agreed to children on our first date."

"Yes, I agreed to children, but I never said I wanted to have one right away. And I certainly wasn't planning on leaving my job so soon. I thought I would have another year or so."

"Well, I want to start now. I want to be young enough to be able to keep up with their energy. As far as your little job goes, I'd prefer you got used to staying home all day. It's going to be a big change for you."

She was awed by how much and how quickly he had changed. He went from being an active listener and someone she had become dependent on to give her advice, to a cold, uncaring man who wouldn't allow her to even voice her opinions anymore. She was interested in having a child soon, but she also wanted to have a say in when it happened. She believed it should be a mutual agreement between the two of them, not just one of them stating they were ready and that was the word of the law. What happened to the partnership that Maxwell had been preaching about before they got married? That was what she was excited about. But it seemed that recently, whatever he said, went. There was no partnership, it was him who ran the household, and that household was once Kathleen's home.

"Will you give me a few days to think about it? This is a really big decision."

Maxwell glared at her and shook his head. "You're acting ridiculous. You and I both know you're going to give in anyway."

Distorted Perception

In her heart, she knew he was right. She just didn't want him to win.

After a few weeks, she did give in. She had thought about Maxwell's proposal while she was at home, she thought about it while she was at school and tried to imagine if she would miss it. She thought about what she would do to fill her days between when she left school and when she actually had a child. She hoped Maxwell would accept her response if she told him that she would be willing to leave at the end of the school year. It was only seven months away and it would give them plenty of time to try for a child and she could still work even if she was pregnant. If she ever wanted to go back to work at some point, she didn't want to burn any bridges on her way out. She thought leaving at the end of the year would give the school plenty of time to find her replacement. She didn't think she could bring herself to leave the kids during the middle of the year. After all, the children were the main reason she loved her job.

Maxwell just shook his head as she gave him her answer. She thought she had sound reasoning for wanting to stay through the school year. He disagreed. He told her he wanted her to leave during the holidays so they could start the New Year in the right way. The right way, meaning his way. And he wouldn't budge on his opinion.

When Kathleen tried to argue, he threatened to leave her for not valuing his opinion and desires. Kathleen thought she could argue the same since it would be her career and her body that would feel all the effects. Worried that he may keep good on his threat, the next day, she reluctantly brought a letter of resignation into the school with her. She thought it was the hardest thing she would ever have to do. She loved her job, she loved the children, but she also loved her husband.

It was a bittersweet ending for her teaching career for the foreseeable future. She was afraid to leave, she was sad, but she was also excited about the possibility of having a child of her own. Three days after she turned in her resignation she started to feel better about the situation. The apprehension she had felt began to subside and she had to talk herself out of jumping on Maxwell when he got home from work. Now that the plan was in motion, she wanted a child more than ever.

One week before Christmas she went to the city to buy Maxwell his gift. She stopped for a coffee and paid for it in cash and then made her way into the shops. Maxwell didn't have much as far as what most people would consider "toys," so she had decided to get him a new outfit and a fancy pen for work. When she entered the first shop, she was overwhelmed by the amount of writing implements. She had never shopped for anything like that and figured she would have maybe five to choose from. There were hundreds of them. It took her almost three hours to find the one that she wanted and could afford and she picked out a pair of cuff links that matched it. She hadn't budgeted for the cuff links but Maxwell always wore a suit on days that he went to court and she thought it would be a nice surprise. The salesman boxed and bagged her purchase and ran her card through. He handed it back to her while shaking his head and told her that it was declined.

Kathleen felt the heat rise in her cheeks. "It can't be. That card has no balance on it. Can you try it again, please?"

The cashier did as she requested and shook his head again as he handed it back a second time. She tried all three of her credit cards and none of them worked. She couldn't believe it. She had to ask the cashier to remove the cuff links and she paid for the pen with her debit card. That was almost all the money she had available in her checking account. She thanked the salesman and told him she would come back for the cuff links after she figured out what was wrong with her cards. She left the store and texted Maxwell when she got back to her car.

None of my credit cards are working.

She was halfway home before she got a reply.

I shut them off.

Kathleen was so struck by what she had read she almost drove her car off the road. Bits of gravel struck the bottom of her car and she had to jerk the wheel to straighten out. Her heart pounded and her body shook. She didn't know if it was because of her driving or because of the shock of him turning off all of her credit cards without her permission. She was so angry at him she wanted to scream. What gave him the right to do that? What if she had an emergency and she needed money?

When Maxwell walked in the door that evening Kathleen exploded. She threw questions at him faster than he could answer them. She started screaming that he had no right to turn off her cards. She wanted to know who he thought he was to do such a thing and why he didn't tell her about it. Did he have any idea how embarrassed she was when every single card that she owned got declined? She had never felt so small. Maxwell's amused look made her even angrier. He just stared at her with a smirk on his face like he was enjoying every moment of it. When she made a comment about him having no right to meddle with her finances his look of amusement changed to one of anger.

He growled at her, "Oh, but I beg to differ. We only have one income now, remember? You quit your job. I think I have every right to do whatever I please with my money since I'll be the only one paying the bills."

"You made me quit my job," Kathleen spat back.

The back of his hand advanced so fast Kathleen didn't have time to react. Her shoulder slammed into the wall. Her face stung and her right eye began to well up. It took her a moment to realize what had happened and she was stunned into silence.

Maxwell's eyes burned into her. "You might want to try that again. I didn't make you do anything. I asked you to quit so you could raise our children and take care of our household like a proper wife should. You're the one that made the final decision. But now, since I am the one paying your mortgage, your car payment, and putting food on your table, you will treat me with respect. And don't ever speak to me like that again."

Kathleen felt like a child, trapped. He loomed over her and bits of saliva hit her face as he spoke. She wanted to lash out, scream at him that he was the one who wanted a partnership, he was the one that wanted her to leave her job, but she couldn't. She slid down the wall with her hand covering her swelling face and cried silently while she tried to come to terms with what had transpired. She couldn't believe this had just happened to her.

She stayed in her crouched position for a long time, only straightening up when she heard Maxwell yell from the other room. "You do know that dinner should be waiting for me when I get home, right?"

Kathleen let out a nervous guffaw and immediately covered her mouth, praying Maxwell didn't hear it. She wiped the tears from her face and stood slowly. After all this, he's worried about his dinner. She went into the kitchen and started to pull out pans from the cabinet and food from the refrigerator. Her head started to clear as she was cooking. This was one of her hobbies and she always used cooking as a way to unwind when she felt stressed. She couldn't help but wonder how she was supposed to have his meal ready for him when she never knew when he would come home. She had wasted hundreds of dollars' worth of food in the time that they had been married either because he came home too late to eat or he didn't come home at all.

She served Maxwell dinner in his office. His office, her former storage room, and the room that would eventually become the nursery. She sat by herself at the kitchen table. She only took two bites before she dumped her own food in the trash can. She didn't feel well. Her face hurt and her stomach was in knots. She washed all the dishes except Maxwell's because she didn't want to go in to collect them. It was still early in the evening but she had had enough of the day. She grabbed an ice pack from the freezer and closed herself in their bedroom with a book. She hadn't realized, until she tried to concentrate on the words, how much her eye had swollen up. It was a good thing she had the next day to try to recover before having to go back to her last week of work. She put her book down and covered the entire right side of her face with the ice pack. She cried herself to sleep.

When she awoke the next morning Maxwell was already in his office. She had no idea if he had even come to bed. She put some coffee on and washed the dishes that he had set in the sink while she waited for it to brew. When it was done, she sat down at the kitchen table with her mug and booted up her laptop so she could check the news. Maxwell emerged a few minutes later.

"I thought I smelled coffee." He smiled at her and bent to give her a kiss on the forehead. Kathleen flinched when he bent near her. All she could do was attempt to smile but her efforts failed miserably. Maxwell poured himself a cup of coffee and turned to her. "Hope I didn't wake you. You looked so comfortable I thought I'd let you sleep in."

Kathleen imagined she had looked anything but comfortable. She couldn't even open her eye. "Thank you. I guess I needed the sleep." She didn't know what else to say but she didn't really sleep in. It was only now seven-thirty.

Maxwell leaned against the counter, sipping his coffee. "I have to go out today. I'll be back for dinner."

She wanted him to leave. With the way she felt this morning, she didn't care if he came back or not. Still, she decided to play nice. "It's Sunday. I thought you were going to try to get them off now." Before they got married, they spent every Sunday together. With the exception of the first weekend of their marriage, he had worked every one.

"Try being the key word. It didn't work out today. I'll be back later." He bent down again and kissed the top of her head before heading out. He called back from the front doorway "I'm taking your car today," and slammed the door behind him.

'Well, that's just great,' she thought. It was a good thing she didn't have any plans today. Not like she would be going anywhere looking the way she did anyway but it was the principle. She spent the next forty-five minutes tearing apart the house, looking for her cell phone and then realized she most likely left it in the car the previous afternoon. She could kick herself for not remembering it. Now she had no car and no phone. For the third time in as many days, she was so angry she wanted to scream. She felt like she had absolutely no control over her life and it had all become that way in the past few days. What had she gotten herself into?

Chapter IX

It was the end of February and Kathleen was going stir crazy. She needed to get out of the house more often. It had only been a little over a month since she left her teaching job but already she had almost no social contact with anyone. She hadn't spoken to Vicki once since that day she accused Maxwell of hitting on her. The only place Kathleen had been allowed to go was the grocery store and that was only on days Maxwell left her car with her. He began giving her an allowance and a budget that she had to stay within while she was shopping for food. She did currently have her car. She had had it for two days already because Maxwell took his truck on a business trip. Today was day three of Maxwell being gone and when Kathleen woke up, she immediately headed into the bathroom. She had felt awful for days.

She was tired and nauseas. She chalked it up to Maxwell being gone and her being bored. She shuffled into the kitchen to make a pot of coffee and took a deep breath while it brewed. She immediately regretted it, turned around, and threw up in the trash can. All at once, it hit her. Her initial thought was wrong. With her head still hanging over the trash can she realized she was pregnant. She had to be. She changed into a pair of jeans and ran to the store before she even drank her coffee to pick up a home pregnancy test. She ripped open the box as soon as she got home and followed the directions exactly. Waiting for the results was the longest three minutes of her life. She paced back and forth across the bathroom, refusing to let herself look at the test until she was sure the appropriate amount of time had passed. It was worth the wait. It came back positive and she was happier than she ever thought she could be. The results were the best news she had gotten in months. Maxwell would be thrilled. She also thought, in the back of her mind, her being pregnant would make Maxwell become, once again, the man she thought he was when she married him.

Despite how bad she felt physically, she found herself bouncing around the house. She cleaned everything she could find, she looked up baby names online. Kathleen was elated. She found a recipe she thought Maxwell would love and added the ingredients to her shopping list. She needed to leave soon if she wanted to do the food shopping and have dinner ready for him when he arrived home. He was due back today in the early evening.

While she was out shopping, she ran into Ryan Douglas while she paid for her food. He was a history teacher at her school and they had both started during the same year. He gave her a quick hug and they chatted for a few minutes. She filled him in on her months of solitude and he shared the most recent school gossip. While she was excited to see a familiar face, all Kathleen could think about was being able to tell Maxwell her news. She couldn't stop smiling and it took all her strength not to blurt it out while she spoke to Ryan. Before they parted ways, he leaned in and gave her another hug.

Maxwell arrived in town earlier than expected and had some news of his own. He had stopped at the grocery store to pick up a bouquet of flowers for Kathleen but changed his mind when he saw her speaking to a man through the window. He saw how happy she looked, how broad her smile was, and how upbeat she seemed. He also sat there long enough to see the hug and he guessed his news was coming at just the right time. He drove away without getting the flowers.

Kathleen danced around the kitchen while she made dinner. She planned to tell Maxwell the news while they ate dessert. She knew she would have an awful time trying to keep it to herself until then.

"What's wrong with you?" Maxwell asked when he entered the kitchen. He pulled a bottle of water from the refrigerator and drank it all in one gulp.

Kathleen stopped mid stride and looked at him through squinted eyes. She chuckled. "Nothing is wrong with me, Maxwell. I'm just in a good mood."

"Uh, huh. Haven't seen you like this in a while." He sat at the kitchen table and waited for her to sit down before he started eating. Kathleen noticed the gesture and thought it was odd. But the last thing she wanted to do was question him. She wanted to keep him in somewhat of a good mood so they could enjoy their evening together. Before she got a chance to ask him how his trip was, he blurted out, "so, I have some news. I think you're going to like it."

She almost dropped her glass of milk. He never had news. Oh. What is the news?"

He stopped eating and looked at her. He reached out and grabbed her hand like he used to when they were dating. "We're moving. Next week."

"What?" Kathleen cried. "What do you mean we're moving?" She pulled her hand from his.

"Next week we're leaving this house and moving to the country. I bought us a house out there."

Kathleen's mood went from being the happiest she had been in a long time to livid in a matter of seconds. She could feel her body begin to shake. "We can't move next week, Maxwell. I own this house. I'll need to clean it and put it up for sale. It could take months."

"Already taken care of, beautiful. You don't need to worry about a thing."

"It's going to take me weeks just to pack everything." She sounded like she was whining but she didn't care. This was a huge decision. He hadn't even consulted with her and it's her house. She had no idea he wanted to move. And the country? She had never been to the country. Now she would really be by herself. All she had ever heard about the country was that your closest neighbor was usually miles away.

"No need to worry. I hired movers. They'll be here Tuesday."

"Tuesday? Like five days from now?"

Maxwell laughed. "Well, yes. What did you think I meant when I said next week?" He continued eating his dinner like this was a normal conversation they would have on any given day. "This food is good."

Kathleen had lost her appetite. She slid her plate away from her and shook her head. She was upset that she hadn't gotten to tell Maxwell her news. She wanted to make it a joyous occasion for both of them and it had completely lost its appeal. At least for now. She got up and left the table without eating any more of her food. She just wanted some time away from him to process what he told her.

After about five minutes of fighting back tears she went to stand in the doorway. "What do you mean it's already taken care of? Did you sell my house? How is that even possible?"

Maxwell guffawed at her. After all this time she still didn't seem to get it. Her naivety both humored and annoyed him. "You seem to forget rather easily that I'm a lawyer. There are so many things that I can do, so many things that I have access to, it would make your head spin. And yes, to answer your question, I did sell it. Got a pretty penny for it, too." He smirked at her. "Did you make any dessert?"

Kathleen was furious that he had managed to sell her house and she knew nothing about it. She was sure his job gave him access to information like that, but it didn't mean he had to abuse the privilege. How did he even know she bought the house outright, maybe she had inherited it from her grandmother or bought it from someone else in her family? She didn't, of course, and she guessed he had access to that information as well, but this was the first house she had ever owned. She was proud of her house. And considering it was hers, she would have liked to have some say in it and she would love to know how much he sold it for. She decided now was not the time to ask him about specific details, but eventually she wanted to know.

She dropped a plate with a slice of Boston crème cake in front of him. The fork rattled and bounced from the plate to the table. Kathleen crossed her arms over her chest and stared at him. "I know you have access to a lot of information but how did you manage to sell my house without my consent?"

Maxwell straightened his posture. He pulled back his shoulders, puffed up his chest, and smiled so wide it made Kathleen want to slap it off his face. "As a lawyer, I should advise you to read all forms and documents thoroughly before you sign them."

Kathleen squinted and shook her head. "But I never..."

Maxwell howled with laughter as he watched the realization hit her.

Her mouth hung open and she sighed with shame. "Our wedding day." Her arms dropped to her side, her body deflated.

He nodded his head and shoved a fork full of cake into his mouth. "What's yours' is mine."

After having a few days to think about it, Kathleen had calmed down and was open to the idea of moving. She didn't speak to Maxwell for two days after finding out that she had signed her entire life away on her wedding day. She knew she would home school their children anyway so being so far away wouldn't make much difference in that regard. But now, she thought it may be good for their relationship to be further away from other people. Maybe with the child on the way, their relationship would grow strong again. Back to what it was before they got married.

When Maxwell came home, she told him that she was excited about moving. Not that she had much of a choice since the movers were scheduled to be there the next day. Maxwell seemed glad that she was now receptive to the idea.

On Tuesday morning, Kathleen woke to the sound of beeping in her driveway and groaned. She had hoped the movers wouldn't show up until later in the morning. She crawled out of bed and over to the window. When she looked out, she saw a tow truck hooking up her car. She made her way to the kitchen hoping Maxwell was still home. She had no idea why they were taking her car but she figured he had something to do with it. She laughed to herself at the thought that he had probably sold that too.

Maxwell was sitting at the table when she came in. She looked at him and he glanced at her. She knew immediately that her thought was not wrong. "So, I guess I don't have a car anymore either?"

"You won't need it." He stood, set his coffee mug in the sink, and kissed her forehead before leaving the room.

All Kathleen could do was laugh. She was mad, but there was nothing she could do about it. And maybe he was right, depending on how far out they would be, she may not need a car.

Chapter X

Kathleen had slept most of the car ride to the new house. She didn't feel well and the motion of the car made her ill. When she awoke, she was awed by the amount of open land around her. She had heard the term "rolling hills" numerous times but had never understood what it meant until now. She watched out the window as miles and miles of fields flew past. This was nothing like what she had seen in movies.

"Different, huh?" Maxwell asked.

"Very. I've never seen anything like it." When she looked at the clock, she realized they had been driving for almost four hours. Maxwell seemed to be in an okay mood so she decided it would be a good time to ask him again about his job. "So, I'm just wondering. Um, we've been driving for a long time. What are you supposed to do about work? This is awfully far away from the city." She stared at him, trying to see some sort of tell on his face. She had no idea what she was looking for.

"This is why I'm gone for days at a time. It's a long drive to get out here. There are a few towns in the area, within a reasonable drive from where we are now. And there's a city about an hour and a half from where we'll be. I was on leave from work because I'm working for another firm out this way."

"Oh." Her shoulders sagged and she turned to look out the window. "I guess you could have told me that at some point but that makes sense."

"Yeah, so I could do all my research and paperwork and stuff from the office back home, they were nice enough to let me, but when I needed to meet with clients or go to specific areas, I had to come out here." His facial expression didn't change once while he spoke so Kathleen assumed he was telling the truth. She didn't understand why he couldn't have told her that over the months that they had been together but at least he told her now. And it did make sense why he would want to move all the way out here.

She noticed while they were speaking that she hadn't seen a single house since she had woken up and they had easily gone twenty miles. "Are there any other people out here at all?"

"We'll have a few neighbors. Give it a couple of minutes. You'll see some houses."

They continued driving for another fifteen minutes before Maxwell turned onto a dirt road that Kathleen didn't even see until they were on it. She had to ask him to pull over once and she threw up on the side of the road. She wasn't used to the rocking sensation that the dirt road caused in the car. Once she was settled back in they drove another five minutes before they turned yet again onto another dirt road that looked to Kathleen like it was only one lane.

"This road looks awfully narrow."

Maxwell chuckled. "Well, we're not likely to run into any other cars out here. If we do, those people are trespassing."

"Oh, is this private land that we're driving through?" She felt like she was in another world.

"You could say that. It's mine." Maxwell looked at her for the first time since she had been awake. "Wow. You look like hell."

"Um, well, thank you. For that. I'm not used to these bumpy roads. It's making me sick." Kathleen still hadn't told him about the baby and she was unsure whether it was morning sickness, motion sickness, or the combination of the two. Kathleen felt like she was going to be sick again but did her best to keep the feeling at bay. It was another five minutes before she saw the first house. Her heart thumped as a few more came into view.

"See. Neighbors." Finally they came to a house that sat all by itself. Maxwell pulled into the driveway and stopped the car. "We're home."

Kathleen immediately opened the car door and threw up more than she had eaten that day. This time, she knew it wasn't morning or motion sickness. She was half expecting someone to jump out with a video camera to tell her she was on a prank show. She had never seen a house in such disrepair. She took a lot of pride in her home and the land surrounding it. But this? She didn't know if she would ever be able to fix this. The lawn wasn't mowed, the steps to the porch were crooked and falling apart. The porch itself was missing more spindles than were present. There was a window with a crack going clear across the entire pane and it looked as though the entire house was constructed of nothing but wooden planks. There was no paint, no varnish, nothing. Kathleen could only imagine what the inside of the house must smell like and how damp it gets inside when it rains.

She looked around at the surrounding houses. She was extremely happy that they did have close neighbors within walking distance but those houses didn't seem to be much better than her own. Maxwell got out of the car and started walking the rest of the way up the driveway. Kathleen scurried out of the car to catch up to him. When he opened the front door and stepped inside she wanted to cry. She had a fleeting hope that the inside of the house would look better than the outside. It didn't. There was only one open room. It looked to be a living room, dining room, and kitchen combination. And there was one hallway as far as she could see from the doorway. It smelled almost as bad as she had imagined it would. She figured it had been closed up for years and would need at least a few days to air out.

She stepped in and immediately tried to open a few windows, even hitting them with the side of her fist. They didn't budge. She wasn't worried about the lack of screens or how cold it was outside, she needed to get the musty smell out of the house. She made her way toward the kitchen and took note of the cabinet doors that looked like they were hanging by only one hinge, the chipped counter tops, and the stove and refrigerator that looked like they were from the nineteen-seventies. They both had the coloring of split pea soup. Still on the verge of tears she turned to Maxwell. "Please, please tell me you have repairs in the works. This place looks like it's ready to fall apart. How are we supposed to raise a family here?"

Maxwell glared at her and Kathleen took a step backwards and bit her bottom lip. "How are we supposed to raise a family here?" Maxwell laughed loud and hard but there was no humor behind it. "Now, that is an excellent question. I think, and feel free to disagree with me, the first step to raising a family here would be for you to finally admit to me that you found out you were pregnant a week ago and have neglected to tell me." His words echoed throughout the empty house and Kathleen started to shake.

Her voice wavered as she quietly asked, "how did you find out?"

"Because, you stupid bitch, you left the pregnancy test in the trash can. I saw it when I came home last week." He raised his voice once more. "As a matter of fact, it just so happened to be the same day I saw you talking to your boyfriend at the grocery store." Maxwell advanced one step toward her. Kathleen backed up and slammed her back into the refrigerator.

"My boyfriend?" She had to pause for a moment to figure out what he was talking about. She chuckled from both amusement and fear. "Maxwell, the man that I was talking to was another teacher from the school that I worked at. I only ran into him there."

"Really? You ran into him there? That's why you're hiding your pregnancy from me? That's why you were hugging him? Because you ran into him there?"

"I wasn't hiding anything. I went to the store that day purposely so I could make you a nice meal. I was planning on telling you while we were eating dessert. But that was the night you told me during dinner that you sold my house and I was so upset. I wanted our pregnancy to be a joyous occasion for both of us. I wasn't feeling very joyous after you told me we were moving."

"That's bullshit and you know it. But at least now I won't have to worry about you running off with anyone while I'm at work. You don't have a car and there is no cell phone reception out here. I don't know about the paternity of this kid but I'll damn well know the paternity of the next one." He turned and walked out the front door, slamming it behind him.

Kathleen sat on the floor and dropped her face in her hands. The tears flowed freely and her entire body shook. She was thankful that he walked out instead of hitting her like she feared he would but she was devastated that she didn't get to tell him the news. And she couldn't believe he didn't think the child was his. This wasn't what she expected to happen. She had her hopes set on this move bringing them closer together. The thought of him not believing that it was his child kept circling in her mind and she knew she was going to be sick again. She stood up and ran, doubled over, to the front door and barely made it to the porch railing in time to retch over the side.

When she was done, she straightened up and noticed that Maxwell had left a few blankets and their pillows on the porch. The movers were not expected to deliver their stuff until the following afternoon. Their stuff. Kathleen looked inside the door and wondered if even half of their belongings would fit in such a tiny space. She grabbed the bedding from the porch and made her way back inside. She was tired and knew she could use the rest so she made her way down the hallway checking all the doors to see where the master bedroom was. All three rooms seemed to be the same size so she chose the one at the very end of the hallway and laid the blankets out on the floor.

She had no idea what time it was when she fell asleep, only that the sunlight had begun to fade. When she awoke, the sun shined brightly through the lone bedroom window and she squinted against the bright light. Her body was stiff from sleeping on the hardwood floor but her mind actually felt refreshed. She guessed she had somehow slept for close to twelve hours.

Kathleen had no idea if Maxwell had come home last night or not but when she walked into the main rooms of the house she saw that his truck was not outside but there was a can of coffee and a coffee maker on the counter. She didn't look nor did she care if there was any milk to put in it. She was just grateful she had that much. She knew she shouldn't be drinking coffee because of the baby but that would be the hardest transition for her. She had cut down to only one cup per day since she found out.

She took her mug and went out the back door to see what the view looked like. It was cold out. Her breath fogged up in front of her and goose bumps prickled her skin as she shivered. The first sip from her mug warmed up her insides. She still had no idea what time it was but she hoped it would warm up a bit as the day went on. If Maxwell wouldn't be home she figured she might as well go and introduce herself to a few of her neighbors. She had a feeling that since she had no way of going anywhere she would be spending a lot of time with them. At least she hoped she would be. Being this far out, she wouldn't have any help with the baby if she couldn't make fast friends with a few of the neighborhood women.

As she made her way back inside, she heard the laughter of children coming from across the field in her back yard. She stepped off the porch and even though they were far away she could see a bunch of children running through the open area. It looked as if they were all different ages and she could hear both boys and girls. Her heart sped up with the knowledge that there was a group of children in the neighborhood and she hoped she would be able to meet them soon. Seeing them having so much fun together made her miss school. Even though it had only been a few months she already missed teaching and seeing the children grow throughout the year.

Once the kids were out of her sight she went inside to shower and make herself presentable. The hot water felt refreshing and made her muscles ease up a bit. It only lasted about five minutes before it started to run cold. She made a mental note to mention it to Maxwell when she saw him next. She brushed out her hair and put on some makeup, giving close attention to the red welt just on the side of her cheekbone. She dressed in the only other outfit she had brought with her, a pair of jeans, a long sleeved shirt, and a light sweater in lilac. She wished she had thought to bring something a bit warmer. The heat was on but there was still a chill in the air.

She stepped on to the front porch and looked down the street in both directions. As far as she could tell, they were the furthest house down the road. She decided to start at the closest house to hers and make her way down the road on one side and then back up the other side until she had met all the neighbors.

The first house she came to looked just a little better than her own. It was the same size but the lawn was mowed and you could tell that someone lived there. A few potted plants dotted the porch and Kathleen could see curtains hanging in the windows. As she approached the front door she noticed the steps to the porch had been fixed crudely but at least she wasn't afraid to step on them like she was her own. She knocked on the door cautiously, afraid she may knock it out of the frame if she hit it too hard. She could hear yelling coming from the back of the house but couldn't make out the words. It didn't sound angry and she assumed it was just to get the kids' attention.

The door swung open and the woman on the other side made Kathleen smile. She had brown, loosely-curled hair, the brightest blue eyes Kathleen had ever seen, and was a little heavier set than she was herself. "You must be Kathleen. I've heard so much about you." She stepped forward and wrapped her arms around Kathleen's shoulders. Kathleen froze. She didn't expect her neighbors to know her name and she was a bit taken aback by such an affectionate display. The woman eased her embrace and stepped to the side. "Come in, come in." She swung her arm to the side as if Kathleen wasn't sure which direction to go. "I'm Janie, by the way. Come, sit down, can I get you some coffee?"

Kathleen wondered how many cups she had consumed that morning given her extreme amount of energy and cheerfulness. "Um, no, I'm okay, thank you."

Before she could tell Janie why she was there she was interrupted. "Are you pregnant?" She let out a hearty chuckle when she saw the surprised look on Kathleen's face. "Okay. Well, I was really joking because I don't trust anyone that doesn't practically live on coffee. But since you might as well have admitted it, how far along are you?"

She was shocked and it took her a moment to find her voice. Was the look on her face that obvious? She stuttered when she tried to speak. "I... I don't really know ex-exactly. I just found out last week and then we moved here. I haven't even had a chance to see a doctor yet."

"Well, don't worry about that." Janie stood by the refrigerator adding some milk to her own coffee and pouring a glass of orange juice. "Maxwell has a wonderful doctor that makes house calls out here. I'm willing to bet he's already made an appointment for the doctor to come and see you." She set the glass of juice in front of Kathleen and sat down. "I know. You probably want to go to a regular doctor, in a regular office like you're used to. But trust me, Dr. Caldwell is the best around. He's delivered all the children that live out here. It's hard being so far away from the city. Dr. Caldwell only lives about forty minutes away so he's really the best option."

Kathleen wasn't sure if that made her feel better or not. She hadn't even considered the fact that there were no doctors around the area. She was so used to being able to drive within twenty minutes and get anywhere she needed to be. "I'm not sure that I would be comfortable with that I've always had female doctors and I do think I'd prefer a clean, sterile office."

Janie gave her a sorrowful look. "Oh, honey." She reached out and patted the top of her hand. "You don't have much choice out here. We're a long way from civilization." They sat in an awkward silence for over a minute. Kathleen had no idea what to say so she just nodded her head and drummed her fingers on her glass of juice. Janie broke the tension. "So... I know you've only been here since last night but what do you think so far? Have you gotten a chance to look around at all? I mean, a field is a field, but there are other things to see."

"No, I haven't. It was a long trip yesterday and I've been a bit under the weather because, you know." She glanced down at her stomach to indicate the baby. "But I've never been to the country before so this is all new to me."

"That's right. Maxwell did mention that you're more of a city girl. This may take a bit of getting used to for you. But, the fields are really lovely to walk through. Especially in spring when the wildflowers start to bloom. And there's a stream that runs across the street from you. It's a wonderful place to visit in the summer. You can dip your feet in to cool off when it's hot outside."

Her mind felt overloaded. Being in the country was completely taking her out of her element. She had never once considered 'dipping her feet in a stream to cool off.' She wasn't even one hundred percent sure she knew what that meant.

"You look like you're going to throw up. Is it morning sickness or just the feeling of being overwhelmed? If it's the first, unfortunately, I can't help you with that. But, if it's the second, just give it a little bit of time. I promise you, it is not that bad here.

It's peaceful, all of us get along, and we have parties and cookouts. Give yourself a chance to get settled, introduce yourself to the rest of the neighborhood, meet the children. You'll find comfort a lot sooner than you think you will."

"Do you have children?" Kathleen assumed the answer but figured she would ask anyway.

Janie nodded her head. "Four. Jacob, Maxine, Wendy, and Michael. You probably heard them screaming through the fields this morning."

This time it was Kathleen who nodded. "I did. I liked it, though. I love children. I was a teacher back home." She frowned at the thought of all the children she had left behind.

"Maxwell had mentioned that." She stood and set her coffee mug in the sink. "Speaking of the children, I should start getting their lunch ready. You're welcome to join us, if you'd like." She began rummaging through the fridge, pulling out meats and cheeses.

"Thank you for the offer but I think I should be going. The movers are supposed to be here this afternoon." She stood and placed her juice glass in the sink.

"If you change your mind, I've got plenty of food."

Kathleen turned to leave and turned back again. "Janie. You said that Maxwell had mentioned that I was a city girl and a teacher. How long have you known about me?"

Janie spun around with a distraught look on her face. "Oh. I, well, I don't know. A week or so maybe."

Kathleen just shook her head. "Okay. Well, thank you for the juice. I'm sure I'll visit again soon. Oh, and feel free to stop by anytime you'd like."

"Thanks. I'll take you up on that."

Kathleen decided to head straight home. She wasn't sure she could handle meeting anyone else today. Since she didn't have anything else to do, she sat on the top porch step and replayed her conversation with Janie. Maxwell had told her that he owned all this land but she thought it was strange, even if they were his tenants, that he would have such detailed conversations with them. She guessed she should be flattered that he talked about her.

She didn't know how long she sat there with the cold air penetrating her body but she stood when she heard the roar of engines coming up the road. Large clouds of dust rose behind the vehicles as they approached. Kathleen raised her hand to shield the sun and as they got closer she could clearly make out Maxwell's truck followed by two moving vans.

She met Maxwell when he pulled into the driveway. She never thought she would be this happy to see all of her stuff. She was starved and wanted warmer clothes and a chair to sit on. Maxwell rolled down his window and handed her a bottle of water and a ham and cheese sandwich. Kathleen had never loved him more than she did at that moment. She stood up on her toes and leaned in the window to give him a kiss. "Thank you. I was so hungry I considered going back to Janie's to take her up on her offer for lunch."

"Ah. I wondered if you would head out and introduce yourself to anyone." He got out of his truck and waved the moving vans forward. The first truck backed all the way up to the porch stairs and the men immediately began moving furniture into their home.

Kathleen ripped the wrapping open on her sandwich and began scarfing it down, taking her next bite before swallowing the previous one. She was worried that it may make her ill but she was so hungry she was willing to take that risk. "Thank you for the coffee this morning" she managed to mumble between bites.

"That wasn't me. It was Allison. I asked her to bring some over for you."

Kathleen stopped mid chew and held up a finger to stop him. She swallowed and asked "Allison? Your sister, Allison? She lives around here?"

"Right up the road. Hers is the house that sits further back from the rest. You should probably think about introducing yourself to her." Maxwell turned and contorted his body around the van so he could get into the house.

Under her breath Kathleen grumbled. "Maybe she should introduce herself to me since she practically broke into my house this morning while I was sleeping." But she was still excited that she would finally be able to meet his sister. And they were neighbors. She had planned on spending the entire next day unpacking and setting up their new house but now she changed her mind. She would take the time to go introduce herself before she did anything else. Then she would do her best to try to make this pile of wood into a home. Staring at it from outside, she knew it would be the biggest challenge she had to face yet. She hoped Janie was right and she would settle in soon.

She followed Maxwell into the house to see where the movers were putting her stuff. She had a feeling she would have to rearrange everything they placed. As she expected, they had all of her furniture wrong. She was always under the impression that they were supposed to have some idea of where to put things. At least the big stuff. As it stood right now, her couch sat in the dead center of the room, facing the kitchen. She had to stifle a laugh when she saw what they had done. Who in their right mind would face a couch toward the kitchen? She was too exhausted at this current moment to care that much so she walked over and flopped down on the couch anyway.

Using the armrest as a pillow, Kathleen tried to come up with a plan for unpacking that wouldn't make her too tired. She already seemed to be getting tired with minimal activity. She decided to unpack the majority of the kitchen boxes that afternoon before going to sleep so she would be able to make lunch and dinner the following day. She had no idea what she was going to do for dinner that night.

The next day, after she went to Allison's, she would work on the bedroom boxes so she could find all of her clothes. They had wardrobe boxes so she wouldn't have to worry about rehanging all of their clothing, all she had to do was open the box and move the clothes from the box to the closet. Until a few days ago, she had never seen a box like that and with the way she currently felt, she thought it was the best invention ever. While she stared off into the kitchen she reminded herself that she needed to find her small toolbox so she would be able to fix the kitchen cabinets. From her current position she could see that every single cabinet door hung at an odd angle and she worried that if she didn't fix them as soon as possible she would try to open one of them and the entire door would come off in her hand. It would be just her luck.

She pulled herself out of her daydream and realized that she had been completely oblivious to what had been happening around her. Had she been sleeping? In the amount of time that she had been planning and thinking about the kitchen cabinets, piles of boxes had appeared all around her. She shook her head to try to wake up a little bit and wondered if this was what people had often referred to as 'baby brain'. She thought it was too early on in her pregnancy for that but she had no other explanation for it. It wasn't often that she found herself daydreaming or being so oblivious to what was going on around her. She had to get up and walk around to try to clear her head further. Even though it was still cold outside, she figured the chill in the air would help her focus a bit. She walked outside and sat on the steps again while trying to stay out of the way of the movers. She had no idea where Maxwell had gone but his truck was no longer in their driveway.

In that moment, it occurred to her that Maxwell had taken at least Tuesday and Wednesday off from work and didn't bother to tell her. She was always one to give the benefit of the doubt so even though she wanted to be angry she assumed maybe he just wasn't used to having to tell anyone. She would have to ask him to fill her in on things like this. She backtracked and wondered if it would be worth the argument. Even though he never said outright that he was taking the days off she should have assumed since they were the two days he had told her they were moving. She decided she would wait until it happened a second time, if it happened a second time, before she said anything. After his outburst yesterday, she wanted to keep him in as good a mood as possible, for as long as she could.

Maxwell returned home shortly after the movers had left. While she cooked dinner, Maxwell hooked up the TV and DVD player. They didn't have much by way of food in the house. Kathleen made a simple hotdog and macaroni and cheese meal and they spent the evening laying on the couch watching movies. She took full advantage of what she now considered the 'normal' Maxwell; when he was being sweet and just overall nice. Kathleen was exhausted but she wanted to enjoy the peacefulness. They finally laid down in bed around midnight.

Chapter XI

When Kathleen awoke the next morning, there was a telling chill in the air. Maxwell had already left for the day. She looked out the small bedroom window and squinted. The glare of the sun reflecting off the surface of the snow was blinding. The corners of the windows were covered in condensation.

She started a small pot of coffee and went in search of her boots and a heavy sweater. If she was going to go introduce herself to Allison today, she would have to make sure that she dressed much warmer than she was able to yesterday. She drank her coffee, took a quick shower, and dressed in a pair of jeans, her snow boots, a heavy, black wool sweater, lightweight down jacket, and a tan plaid scarf. She walked out the door and automatically turned to lock it only to remember that she didn't have a key. She wasn't sure she would ever get used to that. Back home, she would barely go out to her mailbox and back without locking the door behind her. It was how she was raised and a full precaution to the heavily populated areas she had always lived in.

The snow was much deeper than she originally thought, and it was still coming down. When she stepped off the porch, the entire toe of her boot disappeared. She wasn't even at the end of her driveway yet and she already wished she had thought to find a hat while she was digging through boxes. She pulled at her scarf to cover more of her neck and shoved her hands into her jacket pockets. She angled her head down and squinted her eyes to avoid an entire face full of snow. She was never much of a winter person but out here, in the country, it looked beautiful. The only sound was that of the wind blowing the snow around her. Everything else was silent. There were no cars passing by, no children screaming, no birds chirping. It was peaceful.

By the time she lifted her head up she found that she was only halfway to what she was assuming was Allison's house. Maxwell told her it was the house that sat back from the road and there was only one that was noticeably further back than the rest. She put her head back down and continued her trek. It felt like it took her forever to reach her destination. Maybe the houses were farther apart than she thought. She breathed a sigh of relief when she finally found herself in front of the house. She assumed the narrow passage where the snow dipped down just a bit from the rest was the driveway. The door opened when she was two-thirds of the way up.

"Kathleen. Hurry up, honey. You'll freeze to death out there." To her surprise, Allison knew who she was. Kathleen was glad that she didn't have to make some sort of awkward introduction. She knew she must have been quite a sight with her windblown hair and nonstop shivering.

She picked up her pace and when she got to the door, she kicked the snow off her boots as best as she could. She shook her head to relieve it of some of the snow that had accumulated and stepped inside. Allison had stood there and held the door open for her. Her house was much warmer than Kathleen's had been, and she saw she had a fire going in her fireplace. "May I?" she asked, gesturing to the flames.

"Of course." She joined Kathleen and pulled up a chair next to the fire. "I can't believe you walked over here like that. You must be absolutely freezing." She stood to grab a blanket from the back of the couch and wrapped it around Kathleen's shoulders once she managed to shrug out of her jacket. "Anyway, as I'm sure you figured out, I'm Allison. It's really nice to finally meet you." She gave Kathleen the biggest smile.

Kathleen could see that good looks ran in the family. Allison was beautiful. She was what many people, male and female alike, would consider 'perfect'. She was thin and had curves like a Barbie doll. She had long blond hair and blue eyes, and she was taller than the average woman. "It's nice to meet you as well. Maxwell has told me so much about you. I was really bummed that I missed meeting you when you were visiting him."

"Oh, yeah. Me too. But things like that happen when you have kids." Allison cocked her head and grinned at Kathleen. "Speaking of?" She raised her eyebrows and sat in silence waiting for Kathleen to confirm.

"I guess there aren't any secrets around here, are there?" She chuckled and shrugged her shoulders. It made her happy that everyone seemed to be excited about her being with child, but she hadn't gotten to tell a single person herself. Janie didn't count because

Kathleen didn't actually say anything, her facial expression gave it away. "But, yes, I am expecting and I'm so excited about it." She grinned from ear to ear. It was the first time she had gotten to say it out loud. It felt good. It solidified it in her mind.

"I'm excited for you. I'm looking forward to having another baby in the mix." Her face twisted as the words left her mouth. She realized how bad they sounded and wished she could take them back.

"The mix?" Kathleen almost snorted. "What it that supposed to mean?" She was still smiling even though she was confused as to what Allison was referring to.

"Uh, well, you know. Because there aren't many people all the way out here. We all kind of help each other out, you know?" She could hear the insecurity in her own voice and hoped it wasn't quite as obvious to Kathleen.

Kathleen nodded her head. She still didn't quite understand what she meant but it was fine. "Do you have more than one?"

"Mm hm. Believe it or not, I have five. All twelve years and under." She laughed. She couldn't help it when she saw the look on Kathleen's face. "You look terrified."

"No, not at all. You just look...well, you look much too young and too... good, I guess, to have that many kids. And they're all under twelve? Do you ever sleep?"

Allison laughed again. "Thank you and yes, I sleep exactly once a week, for two hours. The kids go to Rebecca's house for dinner on Thursday nights."

Kathleen burst out laughing. She couldn't help it. Allison sounded so serious when she said it. It felt good to laugh. Kathleen hadn't realized how much she needed that. "Wait. So, is it just Rebecca that does that or do you all just take each other's kids sometimes?" She was confused again. Between Janie and Allison that was nine children already. She wondered how many Rebecca and the others had.

"We all do it to give each other a few hours of alone time and it gives us a free day of not having to cook dinner. The kids occupy themselves most of the time, but the younger ones still require a lot of attention. It's not exactly as relaxing as it may seem being a stay-at-home mom. Don't get me wrong, all of us love our children more than anything. But it seems like we spend our lives doing laundry, cooking, and cleaning." She stood and took a picture off the mantle. She handed it to Kathleen. "From left to right that's Cayden, Monica, Jessica, Jacob, and Valerie. These are my little monsters."

"They're beautiful." She smiled as she handed back the frame. "I hope I get to meet the rest of them soon. I'm sure Maxwell told you I met Cayden the same day I met him?"

"He did, and you will definitely meet them all soon. You can't hide from this many kids for long."

"I probably should introduce myself to Rebecca and tell me, who else?"

"Oh, yes. Rebecca is directly across the street from me. And Megan is just a bit further down the road. Samantha is around the corner."

"Huh. I didn't even know there was an 'around the corner'. From my house, I can only see three houses. Yours, Janie's, and I guess Rebecca's. But that makes sense considering all the kids I've heard. I wondered where all the rest of them came from." She had made her way into the kitchen at the back of the house and looked out the window to try to see the house that Allison said was Samantha's.

"There are quite a few running around. Rebecca and Samantha each have a child that were born two days apart. That was quite a week. They're four now and the best of friends. They have seen each other every day of their lives and I don't think they would have any idea what to do without each other."

The last comment made Kathleen's heart ache. She knew exactly how the kids would feel. She missed Vicki more than she was willing to admit. She would give just about anything to be able to call her and say hello. If nothing else, she wanted Vicki to be able to share in her joy at expecting a baby. They had always planned to do it together.

"Well, Allison. I feel like I've taken up a sufficient amount of your morning, but I really wanted to come over and introduce myself. I think I'll be heading home now. I have so much to do. My entire life is sitting in boxes right now. Maxwell will be pissed if he thinks I was just hanging out having tea all day and didn't do anything at home."

"I know that feeling." She nodded her head in agreement. "It was really great to meet you. And I have no doubt that we'll see each other again soon." She gave a smirk and a sideways glance. "Can I get you a hat for the walk home? It doesn't look like the snow has let up at all. I don't want you getting sick, especially while you're carrying the baby."

Kathleen accepted her offer and pulled the knit cap over her head before walking out the door. It felt as if the wind had picked up quite a bit since she had gotten to Allison's. She had to pull up both her scarf and the collar on her jacket to shield her skin from the wind and snow. She was grateful for the hat Allison had loaned her. It was snowing much harder than it was when she had gotten there and with each step her feet were sinking into the snow. It was almost as high as her boots in places, she could feel the cold seeping through the tops of them. Her socks were getting wet, and Allison's words circled around in her mind. She didn't want to expose the baby to any sort of germs, especially since there were no doctors anywhere near here. That reminded her that she needed to speak to Maxwell about what she would do about a doctor.

She had given it quite a lot of thought since speaking with Janie yesterday and she decided she was not comfortable having a doctor that made house calls. She wanted an office or a hospital. A place with nurses and doctors and sterile equipment. Somewhere she could trust the people that were supposed to care for her and her unborn child. It was almost making her angry that he would try to subject her to a house call making doctor. She could feel her muscles tense up and she had to remember that she hadn't even discussed this with him yet, all she had so far was what Janie had mentioned to her. She had no idea if it was true or not. She didn't picture Janie as the type to lie outright like that but then again, she also didn't believe that Vicki would be that type of person either, and she was her best friend. She kicked a huge pile of snow as she walked and realized she was behaving like a child. She had no reason to be mad at Maxwell, she had no reason to believe Janie lied to her. She would just have to ask Maxwell about it tonight. She was at the point where she would have to start seeing a doctor for pregnancy care and she would like to get that ball rolling sooner, rather than later.

When she got home, she made herself a cup of hot chocolate to warm up before she started to unpack the boxes. The dampness in the air had burrowed its way deep into her bones. She had put some clothes away as she dug through them earlier in the morning, so she planned to start in the bedroom. At least that way she would be able to say that one room was completely done. That would make her feel much better and accomplished for the day. She also wanted to make her way into the kitchen before she ran out of energy. She wondered what she would be like a few months from now once she started to put on weight if she already felt this tired just trying to empty a few boxes. It made her want to sit down just thinking about it.

Kathleen made record time putting away the rest of the clothing. She broke down all the boxes and fit them inside each other so they could easily be disposed of. She was over halfway through the kitchen boxes when she decided she better take a break from unpacking to make dinner. Her stomach told her it was nearing that time. The sun had started to set, and she expected Maxwell shortly. Today, she was glad he had a big truck because the snow, even though it had slowed a bit, was still coming down. Staring out the front window, she was thankful she didn't have a car to worry about. She always hated having to go out in the cold to clean it off. She wasn't upset at all that she didn't have to drive anywhere in it. She always felt as though the snow had more control over her car than she did.

As she thought about how happy she was not to have to worry about those things, she also realized how angry she still was about him selling her car without telling her. It didn't matter much now anyway. Even if she had a car she didn't have anywhere to go. And she supposed if she started to go stir crazy, Maxwell would let her use his truck on the weekends so she could go out somewhere.

Maxwell still wasn't home by the time she finished making dinner, she put it in the oven to keep it warm. She continued unpacking the boxes that were left in the kitchen until eight o'clock. It wasn't until she sat down on the couch, with her book, that she heard his truck coming up the road. She got up to get his plate and heard him open the door as she filled his glass.

"Well, I'm glad you thought to clean up the driveway so I didn't have to walk the entire length of it," he grumbled upon entering. His voice echoed through the house.

"Hello to you, too. Dinner is on the table." She walked toward the door to give him a kiss while he took his shoes off but stopped mid stride. She thought he was joking about the driveway but now that she could see his face, she knew he was not entertained. "I...I'm sorry. I thought you were joking about the driveway."

"What is it, exactly, that you think 'taking care of the house' means? It's not just making sure it's clean. It means taking care of all the property the house is sitting on. There is no excuse for me not to be able to use my own driveway when I get home from work."

"We've only been here for two days. I didn't even know if we owned a shovel." She had no idea how he wanted her to respond, but she knew it would be a rough night.

"You managed to make it all the way down to Allison's today yet couldn't be bothered to look in the shed out back to see if there might be a shovel in it? Honestly, Kathleen. Could you use your head?"

"I'm sorry. I didn't even think to look in the shed. I guess I just assumed it was empty. I'll go out first thing tomorrow and see if there's one in there." She smiled but he didn't seem to care.

"Or, you could look now so I don't have to walk through the snow again in the morning. There's nothing quite like having soaking wet feet to start your day."

"Couldn't you just wear a pair of boots until you get to the truck and then change into your shoes?" She immediately regretted having said that and now looked for any reason to get out of the house before things turned ugly. "Uh. Do we have a flashlight?"

Maxwell took a second bite of his dinner and set his fork down. "I'm sure there's one in a box somewhere. I'm going to bed." He stood and brushed past her on his way to the bedroom.

Kathleen's body sagged with defeat. She wanted to yell and cry at once but knew she didn't have time to do either. She scraped Maxwell's uneaten dinner into the trash can and put the plate and glass in the sink. It took her almost an hour to find a flashlight in one of the boxes in the guest room. She pulled on her boots and bundled herself tight in a jacket, scarf, and the hat Allison had loaned her. The snow was deep, she was already panting by the time she reached the shed. On a normal day this mission would wear her out and she thought maybe Maxwell had forgotten that she's pregnant.

She struggled with the door of the shed; the weight of the snow was holding it firmly in place. When she felt it finally budge, she closed her eyes and prayed that there was no shovel to be found. To her dismay, when she shone the flashlight into the shed, it was there, standing against the far wall, right in front of the door. "Shit," she cursed. She was already chilled to the bone; she knew it would take her all night to shovel out the driveway.

As she made her way around the house she swore again. She had forgotten there weren't any lights in the front of the house. Although the snow lightened what would ordinarily be pure darkness, she still couldn't see nearly as well as she needed to. She stood the shovel upright and leaned against it while she tried to figure out what to do. The batteries in the flashlight wouldn't last for long and she couldn't hold it and shovel at the same time. After a few minutes of contemplating, she decided to make two trails. She shuffled her feet down one side of the driveway and shuffled back up the other side to create a guide for herself. It wasn't the whole driveway, but it would give Maxwell a clear path, wide enough to walk down. She took a moment to admire her work and then turned off the flashlight and grabbed the shovel.

After nearly an hours' worth of work, she took a quick break. Her back was sore, her hands were already blistered, and for the second time that evening she felt defeated. Looking back at what she had done, she realized she had only shoveled about one-third of the driveway. Her fingers and toes were completely numb and she had no idea how she would make it the rest of the way. The snow was heavy, it was deep, and she was already exhausted. She sighed and gave herself a pep talk about how the sooner she got started, the sooner she would be done. It was the same talk she had given a hundred times to her students.

She threw the last shovel full of snow off to the side and dropped into the bank she had created. It was four o'clock in the morning and the few body parts she could still feel were like jelly. She stood and dragged her feet as she walked back to the house. She removed her boots, jacket, and mittens and collapsed onto the bed with the rest of her clothes and hat on. Kathleen was asleep almost before her head hit the pillow.

When she awoke, she felt like she hadn't slept at all even though it was after nine. She couldn't remember the last time she had slept that late. She shuffled her way to the kitchen with her eyes half closed and filled the coffee pot. While she waited for it to brew, she sat at the table with her head resting in her hands. When the pot gurgled to tell her the coffee was ready, she opened her eyes and saw a piece of paper laying on the edge of the table. She lifted it and read the note:

Kathleen,
It might be useful to introduce yourself to Megan to ask her if you can borrow the snow-blower. It will make it easier for you to put the shovel back in the shed.

Kathleen slammed her fist down on the table. "Son of a bitch", she cried. She was so angry her body shook. Her muscles were screaming, and she was exhausted. She didn't know she had access to a snowblower. She could have had the driveway done in an hour. She had no plans nor desire to go and meet anyone new today. Her plan was to focus on getting the rest of the house unpacked so she could spend her time decorating it over the weekend. She wanted to put up her pictures, fill her bookshelves, and put up her trinkets so it actually felt like home. Now, not only did she need to be sociable, but she needed to spend her time snow-blowing the yard so they would have a path to the shed. She wanted nothing more than to curl up in a ball and go back to sleep.

She showered and put on some warm clothes. If she had to spend more time outside, it would be best to do it while the sun was shining. It may not exactly keep her warm but the sunshine itself would at least make her feel better. She was not looking forward to the walk in the cold, Megan's house was far away. During the summer it would probably be a nice stroll but in the dead of winter it was much too far to be comfortable. It had finally stopped snowing at some point after Kathleen had gone to bed, but the wind still blew the snow all over and she had to keep adjusting her scarf to stop it from blowing down the front of her jacket.

When she reached the end of her driveway, she noticed that someone had come and cleared the road and assumed it had been done yesterday since Maxwell was able to get his truck all the way to their house. Even with the roads cleared, it had taken her almost fifteen minutes to walk the distance to Megan's house. The snow was slippery, and she kept having to slow down because every time she picked up the pace, her feet started slipping out from underneath her. She knew it was probably early on to worry about such things, but she was afraid for the safety of the baby if she fell.

It had only been a week since she found out, but every thought she had somehow turned to thoughts of the baby. How would it affect the baby? Is it bad for the baby? Does she know how to care for a baby? As excited as she was, she couldn't help but wonder if this is what it would be like for the rest of her life; just one continuous stream of constant worry.

As she turned into the driveway, she could hear faint laughter and shouting coming from off in the distance. She hadn't seen a single child on her walk over, possibly because she had her head down, but she wondered where they were all hiding. She glanced around but couldn't see anyone. The front door of the house swung open and Megan boasted. "Kathleen. I'm so glad you finally found your way down here. Come in, come in. You look half frozen. Come thaw out and I'll make you some tea." She headed toward the kitchen and left Kathleen at the door to let herself in. "I was wondering when I would get to meet you, but I thought the weather might keep you away for a few days. It is bitter out there. And that wind. No, thank you, I'll stay inside if you don't mind."

Kathleen had just gotten into the kitchen and hadn't had a chance to get a word in yet. She only thought Janie was talkative, she had nothing on Megan.

"So, Kathleen. Tell me, how do you like it here so far? I know it's very different from what you're used to, but I think you'll love it once you settle in. How are you feeling with the pregnancy? Are you sick yet? Yes, we all tell each other everything." She took a breath and laughed heartily. "I'm so sorry. I talk a lot. You can interrupt me any time you want. I promise, I won't be offended."

"Um," Kathleen chuckled. "Well, I'm glad I finally got to meet you, too. I am frozen and I very much appreciate the tea. I've only met Allison and Janie so far. I really liked both of them so that makes me feel better about being here, knowing that I have friendly neighbors. And I do enjoy the solitude. I'm not used to everything being so quiet, but I think I'll also feel much better once I get the house unpacked and make it more like my home. And yes, I am very sick and exhausted. I'm doing my best not to let it bother me because I'm also really happy to be carrying a child." She smirked. "Did I miss anything?"

Megan laughed. "Nope. And I'm really glad to hear that you like Janie and Allison. I think you're going to fit in nicely here." She handed Kathleen a mug of tea and watched as she gripped it with both hands to thaw her fingers. "I have the snow-blower all ready to go for you. I had Danny, that's my son, get it out this morning just in case you showed up. He can probably bring it to the house for you, if you'd like. Speaking of, the kids should be home for lunch anytime. You're more than welcome to join us. It's nothing fancy, just egg salad sandwiches, but we have plenty."

"How did you know I needed...oh, never mind. I don't want to know. Thank you, and I may take you up on the volunteering of your son to bring it to the house. I would also love to join you for lunch if it's not too much trouble. These days, it hits me all at once. When I'm hungry, I'm really hungry."

"Oh, how I remember those days." Kathleen heard peals of laughter. It sounded like a hundred kids ran past the side of the house. The back door swung open letting in a huge gust of freezing cold air. "Stop!" Megan yelled. "Boots off outside, hats and mittens on the radiator. And hang up your jackets."

The three children that Kathleen could see all grumbled as they backed out of the house and began kicking their boots off. She watched one pink boot go flying past the window and giggles erupted from outside. Kathleen had to stifle a giggle herself.

The children were introduced as they came through the door. "This is Danny. He's my oldest. Patsy is the middle child. And the youngest, back there, is Brooke. Eleven, seven, and five. This is Kathleen. She's the one that moved in down the road."

"It's nice to meet you all."

All three children mumbled a reply. Each one had pink, wind burned cheeks and they all sniffled from the cold.

"Go wash your hands and I'll get lunch ready." She started to pull the bread and egg salad from the refrigerator. "My children are crazy, but I love them."

"They all seem very well behaved to me. They just have about eighty times the amount of energy I do."

Megan nodded her head in agreement.

"Can I help with anything?" She began to rise from her chair and Megan turned and glared at her.

"No, you cannot. But I thank you for the offer." She turned back to the counter and opened the bread. "Honey, I shouldn't say this because I don't really know you but... have you seen yourself? You look exhausted. I know it's been a long, busy couple of days for you, but I really think you need to take it easy. Your body is going through enough right now. When it tells you to rest, you really need to rest."

"I feel like I should be offended by that but I'm not. I appreciate your honesty. The past couple of days have just been non-stop. I'm surrounded by nothing but boxes in my house and I'd feel guilty if I sat down to relax for too long. Plus, I think I would be able to relax more once I get to a place where it actually feels like home, you know?"

"Well, remember, we all pitch in to help each other so if you need anything, all you have to do is ask. And don't be shy about it because we'll do the exact same thing to you."

Kathleen laughed. She could hear the kids yelling and she guessed they were pushing each other down the hallway. They ran back into the kitchen and claimed a chair for lunch. Megan served them all with sandwiches and a glass of milk.

Kathleen took one bite of her sandwich and as soon as she swallowed she knew it was a bad idea. Megan must have seen the look on her face and calmly pointed down the hall. "Same place as your house. I'll make you some soup instead."

Kathleen half ran and half stumbled down the hallway. She dropped to the floor and hung her head over the toilet. When she thought she was okay, she stood and rinsed off her face. She felt awful about what had just happened but at least she made it all the way to the bathroom. That would have been a fantastic introduction to the kids and as a first impression to Megan. She seemed to understand and that much made Kathleen feel a little better.

She took a long look in the mirror. Megan was right, she did look like she was walking around half-asleep. Her skin was so pale it looked almost translucent and she had deep bags under her eyes. She made her way back to the kitchen and saw a bowl of noodle soup sitting in place of her sandwich. She was thankful but also afraid to try it.

"Don't worry about it. Sometimes you have to try a few different things before you'll figure out what will work. And it won't always be the same. If the soup doesn't work, we'll see if you can eat a cucumber." Her smile was genuine and Kathleen was relieved.

"Thank you. I really do appreciate it. I just feel so bad about wasting your food."

"Honey, I have three kids of my own. I've wasted way more than my fair share."

Danny walked back to the house with Kathleen. The trip didn't seem nearly as long with a companion. He pushed the snow-blower and Kathleen asked him questions about how he liked living in the country and what they did for fun. She learned that all the kids were out on the pond when she arrived at Megan's house earlier.

"We were having a snowball fight." He looked over and saw concern on Kathleen's face. "Don't worry. We always divide the teams up evenly to make it fair. We have a mix of boys and girls on each team and have some of the younger kids on each team."

Kathleen was impressed. "Do you always do that or is it only when an adult is watching?"

Distorted Perception

"Oh, always. We'd be in a world of trouble if someone got hurt."

Kathleen questioned the practice of letting the kids out on the ice all by themselves, especially the younger ones. Wasn't anyone afraid that something might happen? Even if it was something small, Kathleen couldn't even see the pond from the house. How would anyone get help in time? She made a note to ask about that the next time she visited someone.

When they got back to her house, Danny asked if she knew how to use the machine and she told him she did. He offered to help her with some of it but she declined. She was impressed by the maturity level of the eleven-year-old. She knew exactly no children that age that would have asked if she needed help or offered to show her how it worked. Megan was doing something right with raising her children and Kathleen wanted to be around her more often to see if she could pick up some of her parenting skills.

Kathleen set to work as soon as Danny left. It had only taken her two hours to make a path from the back porch to the shed. She was relieved to be able to go inside and make herself a cup of tea. She couldn't feel her toes and her muscles were not happy with her. After she finished her drink, she took her second hot shower of the day and then focused on unpacking some boxes. She knew she should rest but she also knew she would feel better once she felt more comfortable in the house. That knowledge was what motivated her to keep going.

She took a break long enough to make some dinner and she planned on going right back to emptying boxes but, to her surprise, Maxwell walked through the door just as she finished cooking. "Hi. I didn't expect you home so soon."

"Makes sense why you were making dinner then. I see you met Megan."

"Yes, and all three of her children. Danny is wonderful. Such a pleasant boy."

Maxwell just grunted and sat at the table.

Kathleen had no idea how to gauge his mood today. He didn't seem angry but also didn't seem to want to talk. That wasn't good for her because she needed to talk to him about going to see the doctor. "How was work?"

"Eh. Same as every day. Mostly paperwork, that's why I'm home so early." He talked between bites and Kathleen could tell he probably didn't stop anywhere for lunch because he was putting the food away.

"So, there is something that I need to talk to you about. I know I just found out last week, but I really think I should try to go see a doctor sometime soon. If nothing else, just to see how far along I am and to make sure that everything is going all right so far. I know you said the city is far away, but I thought maybe I could just go to work with you on the day of my appointment and I can hang out until you're done."

"I'm glad you were thinking that far ahead, but don't worry about it. I have an appointment scheduled for you at the end of next week. Doctor Caldwell will be making a visit next Saturday."

Kathleen was disappointed. Everything that Janie had told her was correct. "Maxwell, I'm not sure that I'm comfortable having a doctor come here for that sort of thing. I'd really prefer to be in a hospital or an actual office somewhere..."

"Stop. Your appointment is already set. Dr. Caldwell has delivered all the children that live around here. He's wonderful and I don't want any arguments." He started to tense up. Kathleen could see it in his face. She'd have to be careful.

"But that's one of my biggest problems. Even if he is wonderful, I've never had a male doctor before and I'm not comfortable with that."

"You didn't seem to have a problem with your boyfriend at the grocery store last week," he growled. "I don't want to hear anything else about it. Your appointment is on Saturday." He pushed back his chair hard enough to scrape the floor, grabbed his jacket, and left the house.

Kathleen cried. She couldn't help it. This was not what she wanted. She had no idea how she could convince him to let her go to a real doctor. Once she managed to pull herself together, she collected the plates from dinner and washed them before going back to her boxes. Maybe she would ask Allison how to talk to him in a way that he might understand.

Chapter XII

Kathleen was starting to get worse as the days went on. She was waking up feeling terrible, going to bed feeling awful, and she didn't seem to get much better at any point during the day. She tried her best over the weekend to do something productive but found that she was having to stop and rest every hour or so. Maxwell seemed to be understanding about it except when he was hungry. Otherwise, he didn't say anything to her about lounging on the couch with a book. When she woke up on Monday morning it took her a long time to get motivated. She was run down and as sick as she thought she could possibly be. She showered and had a cup of tea rather than coffee. After she dressed she set out to go talk to Allison hoping to get some information from her. She was also keeping her fingers crossed that the cold, fresh air would make her feel better.

    Allison was thrilled to see her again. She invited her in with open arms and listened intently as Kathleen told her about what was worrying her. She seemed to understand while she was listening. When she began to talk, it was clear that she did not. "I understand the whole 'male doctor' thing but all but one of my children were delivered by Dr. Caldwell. He's wonderful. And I can tell you that Maxwell will not back down on this. If he's already scheduled the appointment with him, there is nothing you can say that will change his mind. He's been friends with Kenneth for a long time. He recommended him to everyone that lives here and the doctor has taken very good care of all of us. I know you may be a bit distraught by it, but do your best to be open minded. I promise you, you'll be in good hands."

This was exactly what Kathleen did not want to happen. She wanted another female in her corner to say that if she wasn't comfortable, Maxwell should be accommodating to her. Especially Allison. She is his sister, after all. Kathleen thought if anyone would be able to convince him otherwise, it would be her. She tried telling Janie about it the first time she met her but Janie was convinced that Dr. Caldwell was an excellent choice as well. Kathleen felt as though she were in a losing battle. She didn't see that she had any other option at this point. Maxwell had made the appointment and she would be seeing Dr. Caldwell on Saturday whether she liked it or not.

She spent the week decorating the house and trying to make it feel more like home. Maxwell was gone for three days, which surprised her. She didn't think he would be leaving for days at a time anymore since they were so close to the city he was working in. It worked to her advantage though as each night someone came over to join her for dinner. Allison came over the first night and they had a lovely evening. She gave Kathleen some tips on where to place some of the furniture so it would give her some more room. On Wednesday afternoon Rebecca stopped by to introduce herself and asked if she and the kids could join Kathleen for dinner. She said she would bring most of the food if Kathleen would provide a side dish. She couldn't argue with that and she was happy that she would get to meet more of the children.

Rebecca also had four children. Kathleen couldn't imagine having that many. She wondered why everyone in the neighborhood had such large families. The only reason she could come up with was that they had nothing better to do out here. As she expected, Rebecca's children were just as well behaved as Megan's were. From what Kathleen could determine Tori was the talkative one, Chad was the protector, Chris was the quiet one, and Susan was the studious one. Kathleen also guessed that Rebecca was the quietest of the women. She was soft spoken and seemed to have to concentrate to find something to talk about. Kathleen took an instant liking to her.

The third night Janie came to join her and all the kids were at Rebecca's for the evening. They had a great time. There was fun conversation, Janie helped her hang some of her pictures, they watched some television together. Even though Kathleen had had a guest every night, this was exactly what she needed. Her night with Janie was just like one she would have had with Vicki a few months ago. It was a time to have some fun and unwind a little bit. With Janie around, she felt completely free of any stress she had been feeling. She hoped this friendship would continue to grow.

Maxwell came home on Friday night and was nice as could be. Kathleen was pleased and she thought it was a sign that maybe he was happy about how she had put the house together and how much work she had done while he was gone. They spent a wonderful evening together. She asked if he would be with her for her doctor visit and he assured her he would be.

"I know you're a little uneasy about having a male doctor but I will be here with you the whole time. I just want you to understand that being out so far from everything, sometimes you have to make sacrifices. What happens if something does go wrong and you need a doctor right away? Dr. Caldwell is less than half the distance than the closest hospital. I don't know about you, but I would prefer to have one doctor care for me the whole time rather than having a random one step in during an emergency."

Kathleen smiled at him. "I guess that does make sense when you put it that way." His words were the proof she needed that somewhere in there, he did still care about her even though he had been having some trouble showing it.

When Dr. Caldwell arrived the next day Kathleen had no idea what to expect. He was short, balding, and quite plump. But he was personable. He greeted Maxwell when he came inside and introduced himself to Kathleen. He asked some basic health questions and inquired about how she had been feeling. He gave her a list of foods to avoid and offered some suggestions for alternatives. He picked up the box that he carried in with him. It looked to Kathleen like a large, heavy laptop. "Okay, Kathleen. Have you ever had an ultrasound before?"

"Uh, no, I haven't".

"Well, this will be a first then." He lifted a bottle out of the case. "I'll need you to lift up your shirt a bit to expose your stomach. I'm going to squirt a little bit of this gel on you. I'm giving you fair warning, it's cold. And then I'm going to use this thing," he held up a little device with a cord hanging out of it, "to rub the gel around. This will allow me to see the fetus and I'll be able to tell you how far along you are. Ready?"

"I guess so." Kathleen laid back on the couch and raised her shirt as she was instructed. She jumped when the gel hit her stomach. Dr. Caldwell was at least right on that account, the gel felt like ice on her skin.

He began rubbing the wand on her stomach while he watched the monitor that was housed in the top of the case. Kathleen couldn't see the screen so she watched him instead. His lips twitched and pursed. He squinted his eyes and opened them again. His head wobbled from side to side for a few moments. "About five weeks," he said as he removed the device and wiped it off with a cloth.

She questioned him as to the date because she had been feeling so bad for weeks already. He informed her that every woman and every pregnancy was different. Some people knew and had effects right away while others didn't know anything for two or three months. She felt better after his simple explanation.

As Maxwell promised, he sat with her the entire time and never said a word. It wasn't until Dr. Caldwell was getting ready to leave that he leaned over and asked, "So, how long do we have to wait until we can get a paternity test?" Kathleen gasped. She couldn't believe he had just asked that. The doctor just shook his head, shook Kathleen's hand, and left.

Kathleen glared at her husband. She didn't mean to yell but she couldn't help it. "Are you freakin' kidding me, Maxwell? Do you have any idea how embarrassing that was for me? What on earth would ever possess you to ask something like that?" Tears were falling from her eyes and her face was bright red.

Maxwell spun on her fast. His voice bellowed from deep in his stomach "How much it embarrassed you, Kathleen? How do you think I felt having to ask something like that? It's okay for you with your little public displays of affection but I'm not allowed to question it?"

Her voice was weak but loud. "I told you I used to work with him. It wasn't anything like..." The room spun and she felt the side of her head hit the wall. Her vision blurred, her knees buckled, and she fell to the floor.

"I'm done talking about it. And so are you." Maxwell walked out the back door.

Kathleen got up cautiously and stumbled to the bedroom using the wall as a guide. She curled up on the bed and cried herself to sleep.

About an hour after the doctor left, Allison and Janie knocked on the door. Maxwell answered it. They told him they had just stopped by to see how Kathleen was after seeing the doctor. Maxwell tried to divert them. "Kathleen is napping. She's not feeling well."

Allison gave him a stern look and turned to Janie. "Janie, do you mind?"

She dropped her head toward the ground. "No. Stop by the house if you want on your way home." She turned and sulked away.

Allison pushed her way inside even though Maxwell was practically blocking the entire doorway. She turned toward him with rage written all over her face. "You hit her, didn't you? In front of the doctor?"

"You know I couldn't do that. He would be required to say something to the authorities."

To Allison, he seemed amused by his own response and it just made her angrier. "Maxwell. This isn't something to joke about. We've talked about this. It's bad enough that you do it at all but you cannot hit a pregnant woman." She wanted to scream but she also wanted Kathleen to continue sleeping. "You know better than that."

"And you know better than to talk to me like this. You want to keep running your mouth? You'll be able to join her."

Allison knew he had the upper hand and she wouldn't get away with talking to him like this for long. "Where are you staying tonight?"

"I'll be at Samantha's."

"Fine. But just so you know, I will be coming back here later to check on Kathleen." She turned and stomped out the door. She closed it gently so she didn't wake Kathleen but she wanted to slam it as hard as she could.

As much as she wanted to be alone, she took Janie up on her offer to stop by because she knew that's what Janie would need. They were at the point where they didn't even bother to knock on each other's doors. They just walked in. When she opened the door she saw Janie sitting at the kitchen table with her face buried in her hands. She knew she was crying and immediately went over and wrapped her arms around her.

After a minute Janie composed herself enough to ask "Is it what we thought? Is she okay?"

Allison straightened herself and swiped at her eyes to stop any tears from falling. "It's what we thought. And I don't know. I didn't see her. But I'm going back later on to check up on her if you'd like to join me. Maxwell will be at Samantha's."

Janie nodded her head. "I'll go with you. I want to make sure she's okay." She grabbed a tissue from the box on the table and wiped her face. "I know I ask all the time but why does he do it, Allison? Why does he do this when he's supposed to love us?"

Allison just kneeled down and hugged her again. "I don't know. I don't think we'll ever know."

As promised, Allison stopped by Janie's house before going to see Kathleen. They walked down the road arm in arm, partially to keep each other warm, but mostly for comfort. They tried knocking on the door but there was no answer. Allison swore and opened the door a few inches. "Kathleen? It's Allison and Janie. Is it okay if we come in?" Hearing no answer, they walked in anyway. Seeing that she wasn't in the kitchen or living room they made their way down the hallway. They wanted to be quiet so they didn't startle her. "Kathleen?" Allison knocked on her bedroom door. "Kathleen, it's Allison and Janie. We're going to come in, okay?" She cracked the knob on the door and pushed it open. "Kathleen?"

She was laying on her side but she raised her head and looked at them when they came in. She didn't say a word.

"Hey. We came to check on you to see how you were doing after the visit with the doctor." Janie's voice cooed and she impressed herself by how it sounded. She was trying hard to keep it together. "Is it okay if we turn the light on?"

Allison reached forward to the lamp on the end table.

Janie gasped when the light came to life. Kathleen's face was red, swollen, and badly bruised. That didn't look like it was from a fist. She sat on the bed and grabbed Kathleen's hand. "Oh my god. Honey, are you okay?"

Kathleen still couldn't bring herself to say anything. She just stared at the two of them like she was a trapped animal.

"I'm going to go get some ice for the swelling." Allison twirled around on the ball of her foot and practically ran down the hallway. She thought she was going to be sick. The bruise on Kathleen's face was by far the worst she had seen. She leaned against the counter for a moment to compose herself before finding the ice pack and dish towel. She was hesitant to even go back in the room but she knew Janie would need a break as well. She took a deep breath, hoping to calm her nerves, and entered the room.

She leaned forward and held out the ice pack to Kathleen hoping she would take it. When she didn't, Allison sat on the edge of the bed and gently touched the towel to Kathleen's forehead.

She flinched. "Hurts," she whispered.

"I know, honey. I know it does. But you need to keep it on there. You have a pretty good bruise."

She let Allison place it on her head again and she wanted to cry. Her entire head hurt. Her face, the sides of her head, her brain, everything was sore, aching, and throbbing.

Allison looked over at Janie and could see that she was pacing back and forth. "Kathleen, have you eaten? Maybe Janie can make you some soup?" She widened her eyes and nodded toward the door, giving Janie her escape.

Kathleen nodded her head and winced. She wished she had thought about what she was doing first. She felt like her brain physically rattled around in her head.

Janie ran out the door. She was so thankful Allison had done that for her. When she got to the kitchen she slid down the wall and hugged her knees to her chest. She could not believe how bad Kathleen looked. She wondered what happened to make Maxwell that mad. She assumed Kathleen must have fallen and hit her head on something for her to have acquired that much damage. After a few minutes, she pulled herself together and found a can of soup in the cabinet. When it was warmed, she poured it in a bowl and reluctantly made her way back to the bedroom.

Allison removed the ice pack and moved further up the side of the bed so she could help Kathleen sit up. She wished she had insisted on seeing her the first time she had stopped by. "We'll get you some aspirin for your head after you eat. Let's make sure you can keep it down first."

Janie and Allison sat on the edge of the bed while Kathleen ate. No one said anything for about ten minutes. They sat in an uncomfortable silence and the only sound was Kathleen slurping at her soup. Janie had to stifle a laugh a few times. The silence was making her uneasy and her nerves were already on edge.

When she was done eating, for the first time, Kathleen spoke. "I need to use the bathroom." The other two chuckled but were relieved to hear her voice.

Allison stood to allow her room to slide off the bed. Kathleen swung her legs over the side and braced herself with her hands. After a moment, Allison asked if she needed help and moved her hand under Kathleen's elbow. Janie did the same on the other side. As soon as Kathleen stood her knees buckled and Allison and Janie had to struggle to keep her upright.

They escorted her down the hall and into the bathroom. Under the lighting in the bathroom they could both see that the bruise on the side of her face and head wasn't her only injury. The white part of her eye was a solid red, her cheek was swollen, and she had a gash near her temple that was matting her hair down with blood. The other side of her face near her jaw was also swollen and bruised. They let her use the bathroom and then Allison went in to help her clean up her head.

Janie went and busied herself in the kitchen. She made herself and Allison coffee while she washed the dishes and cleaned up the table and counter tops. Aside from the dishes, nothing else had to be done but she did it to keep herself occupied. She was trying to get the image of Kathleen's battered face out of her head.

Once Kathleen got back into bed she fell asleep almost instantly.

Allison joined Janie in the kitchen. "Kathleen's sleeping. Stop sweeping the floor and come sit with me for a minute." Janie did as she was asked and handed Allison a mug of coffee. "She looks pretty bad. I got her to talk to me a little bit while I was cleaning her up. She hit her head on the wall."

"Geez." Janie looked down into her mug. "He hit her hard, Allison."

"I know. I talked to him about it earlier but I didn't know how bad it was. I don't even know if he knows how bad it is. I'll try to talk to him again when he's feeling better." She sipped on her coffee and gripped the mug with both hands. "I think we should stick around for a bit to make sure she's okay. I have no doubt that she probably has a concussion, even if it's mild."

Janie just nodded.

Chapter XIII

It was two weeks before Kathleen left her house again. Maxwell had spent just as much time away as he did at home, but she had no desire to ask him about it. She did as was expected and kept the house clean and made him dinner every day, even on the days he didn't come home. Samantha had stopped by a few days after the incident to introduce herself. Kathleen felt bad that she hadn't made her way over to her house yet. She explained away her head injury by making up an excuse that she had fallen while hanging a picture. She could see in Samantha's face that she didn't sell her story, but she stuck to it. No one else had asked her about it, they just helped her when they could.

Kathleen had a headache for three days following and left her bed only to get herself something to eat, use the bathroom, or make dinner. Once the swelling began to go down, she started to feel better and had more energy. Maxwell never apologized or mentioned anything about how she looked. She could only guess it was because he was being nice. The entire side of her face was black and blue, red, shiny, and swollen. For days it hurt to smile, eat, open her eyes, or try to talk. When Samantha arrived on her doorstep, she was hesitant about opening the door. She didn't have an excuse since Samantha knew she didn't have anywhere to go.

In Kathleen's opinion, Samantha was adorable. She reminded her of a China doll. She had red hair that fell in big, spiral curls around her face. Freckles dotted her cheekbones and nose and she had petite, delicate features. Her voice was quiet and childlike, exactly what one would expect when they saw her. She was full of energy and constantly fidgeted even when she was sitting down. Kathleen offered her some lunch and she immediately jumped up to help her.

Megan and Janie visited the day before carrying bags of groceries with enough food to restock her cabinets and refrigerator. She wondered where all the food came from but decided not to ask. In the month she had been there, someone had come over with groceries every week. She assumed that Maxwell went out and bought in bulk for all the neighbors since no one had a car. The thought popped into her head again while she and Samantha were making lunch.

"You, um, you have a few children of your own, don't you?" She stopped what she was doing and turned to face Samantha.

"I do. I only have two. One is still a baby. Ten months next week."

"Can I ask you a question? I don't want you to think I'm being rude or dense, but I'm really curious."

"Of course, you can."

Kathleen took a deep breath. "I noticed that no one has a car here, but people have brought me groceries every week. How do we get food?"

"Allison usually goes out with Maxwell once a week and does all the shopping for all of us. It makes it easier to just have one person go."

"I can understand that." She hesitated before asking her next question. "I, um, well, I haven't been out too much since I got here but I haven't seen any nor heard anyone talk about having a man in their life? Is every woman here single?"

It was obvious that Samantha was uncomfortable. Kathleen felt bad that she had asked. "Maxwell is the only man in the neighborhood. The rest of us just help each other." Samantha kept making her sandwich and never once even glanced up.

Kathleen felt like she was lying to her. "So, none of you ever go anywhere? You just stay in the neighborhood all the time? Doesn't it make you stir crazy? You don't have a car, the only people you ever talk to are the other women that live here and your children? Don't get me wrong, I think all of you are wonderful but what do you do when you want to see your family? Do they ever visit you?" Kathleen unloaded all the questions that were bouncing around in her head and she wanted to keep firing them at Samantha. She also wanted to give her a chance to answer them.

Samantha looked overwhelmed. Kathleen laughed. "I'm sorry for all the questions. It's just that I've only been here a few weeks but now that I'm starting to notice these things, I'm curious about what all of you do all the time."

Samantha kept her answers short and direct. "None of us really have anything to do with our families except for our own kids. And between taking care of our homes and our children, we have more than enough to do to occupy our time. Honestly, you get used to being way out in the boonies, and after a while you don't even think about leaving. It's peaceful here."

Kathleen could see Samantha's body relax after she spoke. She was glad of that but had one more question that she had to ask. "So, the kids? They don't go to school?"

Samantha glanced at her sideways and Kathleen thought it was a look of pure shock. "We, um... we home school them. Well, the other's do. Mine aren't old enough yet.

"Great," Kathleen responded with joy. "I was actually a teacher before we moved out here. I was planning on home schooling my own children when I had them. Maybe I can help out." Helping with schooling would give her something to do with her time, at least until her own baby made his or her appearance.

Samantha just curled up her lips and nodded but didn't say anything more about it. She changed the subject by commenting on one of Kathleen's paintings and the conversation stayed focused on home decor until Samantha took her leave.

As soon as she left, she bolted down the road to Janie's house. She wanted to give her warning that Kathleen was starting to ask questions. Janie was shocked. She didn't expect her to put together the pieces of the puzzle so fast. She was also worried about Maxwell given the type of mood he had been in for the past few days. She wanted to try to keep him away from Kathleen since she was still recovering from the blow a few days before. "Let's go ask Allison what to do. Preferably before Kathleen decides to ask Maxwell."

Kathleen wasn't sure what to make of Samantha's answers. She wanted to believe what she was saying, but her answers sounded rehearsed, like she didn't want to really give away too much information. There was one answer that bothered her much more than the others. If Maxwell was, in fact, the only man in the neighborhood, where did all the children come from?

Allison made her way out to the road to wait for Maxwell to come home. She bundled up in the warmest clothes she could find, having no idea how long she would have to wait. When he pulled up, she ran around the front of his truck and jumped in the passenger seat. "You're not going to be very happy," she told him with a directness that he knew meant trouble. "You picked up a smart one this time. She's asking questions."

"Damn!" Maxwell shouted. His voice filled the cab of the truck. "What does she want to know?"

"Oh, you know. The same as everyone else. Where are all our families? Why aren't there any other men around? How do we keep popping out children with no father? Why don't we go anywhere? Do the kids go to school?"

"Enough," he shouted. "I get it." He slammed his palm on the steering wheel. "It's too early for this." They sat in silence for a moment. "I'll drive you back to your house. I need to make a visit to the doctor."

"Maxwell, she's pregnant," Allison pleaded.

"Kid's probably not even mine."

Now, Allison knew where the rage came from a few days prior. Megan had gone through the same thing, but maybe it wasn't as bad for her because she wasn't expecting at the time. With her, Maxwell just thought that she was interested in another man. Allison didn't want to push her luck, so she didn't say anything in response.

"I'll just get a sedative from the doctor and tell her the truth. If she acts like she wants to run, I'll give her a drink to stop her. It's nothing we haven't done before."

Allison nodded. "Just be careful with her, please? You really did a number on her head."

She jumped out of the truck and heard him say, "she'll be fine," before the door slammed shut. She hated it when he did stuff like this, but she knew there was nothing she could do to stop him. Once he made up his mind, that was it. No matter what anyone tried to do, they couldn't change his thinking.

Maxwell made a brief visit to Dr. Caldwell and then returned home to Kathleen. He waited all night for her to say something to him, but she never brought it up. He didn't want to get too excited about it, knowing it would come eventually, but at least for the time being he had a little bit of peace. The longer she waited to find out the truth, the better it would be for her and the easier it would be for him.

When Kathleen did decide to finally leave her house, she bundled up and set out down the road. She had no idea where she was headed, she just wanted to go outside and get some fresh air. Even though everyone had seen her face over the past few weeks, she still didn't want to go outside with the way she looked. She would have felt too exposed. Today, she put some makeup on and tried to blend it in the best she could to cover up the remaining splotchy patches of discoloration. She knew they would still be able to see it, but it made her feel better to know that she had at least tried.

She trudged through the snow and made her way down to the stream the Janie had told her about. It was bigger than she thought it would be. The very edges were iced over in thin, jagged sheets but the water was still flowing over the rocks in the middle. Even though she was freezing, she brushed the snow off the top of a large rock and sat down. The cold permeated through the seat of her pants but she didn't mind. She wanted to enjoy the tranquility of the sound of the water running downstream. She wasn't used to natural waters. Being as close to the city as she was, the only water she usually got to see was that in a fountain in a park. Janie was right, she could get used to being out here, especially during the summer. She loved the sunshine and imagined it would be beautiful to see once the snow was all melted away.

Kathleen stayed watching the stream for nearly an hour before she realized she could no longer feel her extremities. She took that as her cue to go out and be sociable. She made her way casually down the road to Megan's house. She was the one that Kathleen hadn't seen in the longest amount of time. She thought she would pop in to say hello and then head back out before it was lunch time for the kids. As she got nearer to the house, she saw a vehicle in the driveway and, as she got closer, realized that it was Maxwell's truck. She thought it was odd that he was around during the day but otherwise didn't give it a second thought. She walked up and knocked on the door. She wasn't yet comfortable with walking into their houses without knocking even though most of them did it to her. It took nearly three minutes for Megan to open the door.

When she answered she looked shocked, or guilty, Kathleen couldn't determine which. "Kathleen. Hi." She opened the door wider to welcome her in. "Um. Maxwell is here." She said it like she was relaying information that Kathleen didn't know. Clearly, she could see his truck in the driveway.

"Yeah. I saw his truck. I didn't even know he was around. I thought he went to work."

Megan breathed a sigh of relief with how accepting and calm Kathleen seemed to be and hoped that she didn't hear it. "Maxwell, your wife is here," she yelled down the hall.

Kathleen could hear his footsteps approaching. "Kathleen. I'm glad to see you're out of the house." He gave her a wide, friendly smile.

"I was tired of sitting around all day. The sun was out so I figured I would go for a walk. I didn't know you were around."

"Had to fix the heater in one of the bedrooms. It was on the fritz. Figured I would do it before work so the kids didn't freeze later on."

"That was nice of you. Jack of all trades, I guess."

"Uh huh. I am heading out now. Kathleen, I'll see you later. Megan, let me know if you have any other problems."

"Okay. Thanks again, Max."

When the door closed behind him Kathleen looked at Megan. "Max? I don't even call him Max."

"Oh." She looked taken off guard. "I call everyone by a nickname. Whether they like it or not."

"No, it's fine. I don't mind. I've just never heard anyone call him that." Kathleen thought it was funny more than anything. She had never considered calling him that herself.

Megan and Kathleen talked for two hours before she excused herself and left Megan on her own to get lunch for the children. By the time she got home from Megan's she was feeling a bit ill. She was starving but didn't want to push it. She wasn't quite sure what she would be able to eat. She spent the rest of the afternoon lounging on the couch before she had to get up to make Maxwell his dinner.

Since her conversation with Samantha a little over a week ago, she had asked every other woman who came to see her the same questions. None of them seemed to want to give her an honest response. But the one question she needed an answer to was the one that was met with the most hesitation. Tonight was the night she had decided to finally ask Maxwell outright. She was going to lay all the questions on the table. She wasn't getting a straight answer from anyone and the only reason she could come up with was that they all had something to hide. She was determined to find out what it was. Even if it meant making Maxwell mad again.

Chapter XIV

Kathleen was nervous. Her palms were slick with sweat and there was a lump in her throat. She was unsure of how to bring up the subject with Maxwell. A part of her wished she were able to ask him her questions with some others around in hopes that his response wouldn't be quite so bad. She knew he would take issue with her asking about the others. He's clearly known them all for a number of years even though no one else would outright admit it.

When Maxwell got home, they ate a nice dinner and had a conversation about Allison's children. Kathleen thought that would be a good place to start since he may be more receptive to speaking about his sister than he would be about the other women. Once they were done eating, Kathleen took a few deep breaths and started in.

"Maxwell. I'd like to talk to you for a moment. I was having a conversation with Samantha, and she told me that everyone here home schools their own children. Are there really no schools anywhere close to here?" She knew it probably sounded odd to him since she had been all for home schooling her own children, but she wasn't sure how else to start the conversation so it wouldn't end in disaster.

He knew the questions were coming but he was shocked they came now. He hadn't prepared himself for it before he walked through the door. "They don't have an option for schooling out here. There are nowhere near enough children, and they would have to travel close to an hour to get to the nearest school. But I'm glad you brought it up. I was actually thinking you may be able to assist with the schooling of all the children once you get comfortable out here. None of the other women who live out here have any formal education beyond high school. I told them a while back that you were a teacher and they all seemed receptive to the idea of you helping them out."

"Well, it would have been nice if you mentioned it to me at some point since you volunteered my services. I mean, of course I'm willing to do it, in fact I would love to, but I really wish you would have said something to me before you brought it up to everyone else. What if I didn't want to?"

Maxwell laughed loudly. "Oh, Kathleen. Little, naïve Kathleen. See, you don't actually have a choice. It was the main reason for bringing you here."

She sat at the table in silence, replaying what he had just said to her. Her heart sank and she felt like he had just kicked her in the stomach. That was his reason for bringing her here?

"All right. Keep going, Kathleen. I know you have more to say. Just say it and let's get this over with so we're not up all night. You can have all day tomorrow to process everything."

She so desperately wanted to yell at him but knew it wouldn't end well for her. Instead, she clenched and unclenched her fists under the table. "Okay." She took another deep breath. "Why are there no other men anywhere near here?" She could feel her muscles tensing up as the words came out, her voice was shaking.

Maxwell laughed again. "Huh. I'm shocked. You caught on a lot quicker than I thought you would have. I'll give you credit for that." He stared into her eyes, and she wanted to scream or cry, she didn't know which. He stood and walked around the table rubbing his hands together in anticipation of his own answer. "Why are there no other men around? Do you feel like you need another man here? Am I not man enough for you, Kathleen?"

"Oh, Maxwell. Of course you are. I just find it odd that there are children running all over the place but there are no men here to actually make the kids."

"There are no other men here because I won't allow it. This is my property. I own everything on it. All the houses in this neighborhood? They're mine. Each and every woman you've met? She's mine. All the children you see running around? Also mine."

Kathleen had tears streaming down her face and yet she wasn't sure she was correctly comprehending what he was saying. "Yours?" She finally managed to squeak out. She began sobbing and wiped at her face with the backs of her hands like a child.

"Mine. Just like you are." He leaned down and kissed the top of her head. It was a gesture she would love under normal circumstances. "Everything you can see here belongs to me. It's my property and I do with it what I like. Before you sit here and try to rack your brain about everything that's going on, let me make things just a little bit clearer for you. You are not the first woman to carry my child and you are not my first or my only wife. When you saw me at Megan's this morning, I was absolutely not fixing a heater. But she's a doll and she learns quickly. She knows better than to give out information without my permission. That's why she didn't tell you." He stopped for just a moment to see if Kathleen had anything else to say. When she didn't speak, he did. "So, are we done here?"

Kathleen couldn't speak. She crossed her arms on the table and laid her head on them. He had a feeling the minute he tried to walk away she would call him back, so he leaned against the wall, with his arms crossed, waiting for her to say something. To his surprise, after about three minutes, she stood up, pushed back her shoulders, and stormed past him. He watched her walk down the hall and close the bedroom door behind her. He heard the lock click and took that as his cue that their conversation was over.

He grabbed his jacket and keys and walked out the front door. He was glad he had thought to permanently lock all the windows, and before he left for the evening, he bolted the front and back doors closed. At least he didn't have to worry about her going anywhere. He drove down to Rebecca's house and parked his truck in the driveway. He was thankful he didn't have to walk anywhere in the freezing cold. He was once again free to go anywhere he wanted without having to worry that Kathleen may see him and start asking questions.

When he walked through the front door Rebecca looked shocked. "Maxwell. I didn't expect you tonight. Is everything okay?"

"Fine. She knows." He grabbed Rebecca by her arm and led her down the hallway.

For three days Kathleen never tried to leave the house. She would get up every morning, make a cup of coffee and retreat to the bedroom to read a book. She didn't bother to make dinner, she just assumed that Maxwell wouldn't come home for a while. On the fourth day she woke up and took a shower. She dressed and planned on going to Janie's to confront her about not telling her what was going on. When she tried to turn the handle of the front door it didn't budge. She tried a second time and then began banging on the door and throwing her body into it to get it to open. Her heart rate was beginning to rise, and she was sweating from the effort. She ran to the back door and tried the knob. She screamed when it didn't move. She grabbed it hard and shook it, knowing it wouldn't work, but it made her feel better to try. She tried to open the windows. She started in the kitchen, moved to the living room, and finally the bedroom but couldn't get any of them to move even an inch. She remembered that there was one that was already broke so she ran to it thinking she would be able to throw something through it and she could crawl out. As she got closer, she saw for the first time that it had wire mesh running through it. There was no way she would be able to leave through the window. She was trapped in her own house. Pregnant, scared, alone, and trapped.

    She slammed her fist on the window and dropped to the floor. Tears streamed down her face and her body was shaking. She didn't understand what was happening to her. She hadn't taken the time in the last few days to think about it.

    Now she was thinking about it. She had married a man that she initially thought was perfect. He began abusing her and controlling her life shortly after they got married. He moved her to a place far away from her friends and family. And he had just admitted to her recently that he had numerous children that she had no idea about and multiple wives that she also had no idea about. And now, he had locked her up in her own house, knowing full well that she couldn't go anywhere even if she wanted to. If she were to try to leave, it would take her days to get to any sort of civilization. And even then, she had no money, no car, and no place to stay. She really was trapped. She couldn't go to the police for help because she had nothing to tell them, all they would do is laugh. Her story would be exactly "my husband tricked me" and that would be the end of hope for getting any sort of help.

She was angry with the other women that never let on to what was happening. But she couldn't help but wonder if it had happened to them, too. Did any of them really know what they were getting into? Do they feel as trapped as she did or are they just okay with it? She had heard numerous times from each of them "You'll like it once you get settled in. You'll get used to it." Now she wondered if they were really talking about being in the country or about the entire situation. Would she really ever get used to her husband sleeping with other women that she was supposed to be friends with? The thought made her stomach turn and she struggled to get up before running to the bathroom.

Kathleen had no idea how she was supposed to feel. Her body was tense, her muscles weak. Her heart rate was high, she could feel it thumping in her chest. She wanted to cry and scream and throw up. She wanted to curl up in a ball in her bed, but she couldn't seem to sit still. If she sat down, all she could do was fidget, if she got up and walked around her entire body protested and told her it had had enough. For two solid days she spent her time alternating between sitting, then making a lap around the house. Time seemed to crawl; she couldn't concentrate on anything. She tried reading and after one page she gave up. She tried cleaning and found herself touching one thing in every room and then giving up.

When Maxwell finally came home after a full week of being away, Kathleen set aside her feelings and ran to him when he opened the door. She wrapped her arms around him and held him there for a long time. She was crying but it wasn't because of the anger or betrayal. It was because she was so happy to see another person. She didn't care that it was him or about how much he had hurt her. She was just thankful to have human contact. Somewhere in the back of her mind, she believed that his coming home to her was a sign that he did love her. It was stupid to think that, and she was aware that she wasn't thinking clearly, but it made her feel better to believe it.

As expected, Maxwell was his usual self. He wasn't overly thrilled to see her; he just simply came home. After a minute of dealing with Kathleen latching on to him, he eased her away. "So, I'm guessing there's no dinner ready?" He turned himself away from her to take his shoes off. Kathleen wanted to punch him for that reaction. Instead, she continued to cry as she made her way to the kitchen.

The following week she was locked in every day. On the fourth day, Allison and Samantha came to visit her and Kathleen learned that Maxwell had given Allison a key. She was not pleased about that. She wasn't allowed to leave her house, but he thought it was okay to give someone else a key to get in. She was so angry she wouldn't talk to either of them for the first twenty minutes even though they kept trying to talk to her. They came over with a few bags of food and made themselves at home. When Kathleen finally decided to speak, she lashed out at both of them.

"I cannot believe that every one of you knew exactly what was happening and not one of you thought to say anything to me. Even if I knew, where would I go if I wanted to run? There is nothing around here. Not one of you would want someone to tell you if your husband had other wives or if he was sleeping with someone else? You don't think that's important to know in a relationship?" She stared hard at both of them. Her eyes were narrowed, her lips were pursed. "And you, Allison, you didn't say anything the day you came over and saw that bruise on my face? Do you have any idea how embarrassed I was by you seeing me like that? The very thought of having to potentially tell you that my husband hit me made my stomach ache. Does he do it to all of you too? Is it some sort of initiation for being the new wife or am I just the chosen one?" She had started to cry, her voice caught in her throat. She sunk into a kitchen chair and dropped her head into her hands. She wasn't sure where the questions came from, and she wasn't sure she wanted to know the answers.

To Kathleen's surprise, Samantha was the first one to speak. "Kathleen, we've all been through the exact same thing you're going through."

"That's exactly why you should have told me," she screamed.

"We couldn't. Maxwell treats all of us the same way. We know better than to say anything to anyone. Someone tried that once and...let's just say it didn't end well. But you need to understand that we know what you're going through. The hurt, the confusion, the anger. We've all been there. It wasn't easy for any of us. But you do have us to support you and help you through this. That's why we're here right now."

"Why? Just because you've all been through this before I'm expected to ignore the fact that you all betrayed me and we're going to become the best of friends now? I'm supposed to forgive you because we have a husband in common?"

"No. You need to listen to what we're trying to tell you. We couldn't tell you because we needed to protect you and ourselves. In time, you probably will forgive us and yes, hopefully we will be friends again. This is a hard thing to understand and we're here to help you through it if you'll let us."

"I don't understand what you mean by needing to protect us. Protect us from what? And why didn't you protect yourself, why didn't you protect me, by just leaving?"

"I know this isn't what you want to hear right now, but honey, we all like it here. We don't want to leave. After you give it just a little bit of time, you'll see that we're all very happy. We have support with raising our children, we all have a roof over our head, Maxwell provides for our children."

"Ha!" Kathleen burst out. "He provides for his children? All thirty-five of them?" She fell into a fit of laughing hysterics. She couldn't believe she was hearing this.

"There are not thirty-five children yet, but Maxwell does love every one of his kids. And he loves all of us." She waited a moment for Kathleen to respond. When she didn't, she continued. "You must be able to see how well we all get along. It's different from what you're used to, what we were all used to, but we've adapted to this lifestyle, and I can guarantee, if you ask any of the ladies here, they will all tell you they wouldn't change anything. We like it here and if you just give it a chance, you will learn to like it, too."

"I don't want to learn to like it. I did like it. In fact, I loved it when Maxwell was my husband, and we were expecting our first child. I loved it when I thought I was the love of his life. I loved it when I didn't know that he already had an entire flock of children. I don't love it here. I don't love knowing that he has four other wives. I don't love anything about any part of this situation."

"I know you're sick of hearing this, but you will get used to it. I understand how you're feeling. But we are a family. We're closer than I ever felt to my own flesh and blood family. I promise you, you will love it. And you'll be teaching again. We all know how much you loved teaching. And the kids are all really excited about it. Kathleen, we want you here. We need you here."

Kathleen was so angry. Her skin felt like it was on fire. "It's not like I can go anywhere. That doesn't really leave me with much of a choice, does it?" She stood and made her way to the door. Samantha and Allison both jumped up when they saw her heading in that direction thinking that she may try to bolt. "I'd like you both to leave." They both looked at her and

Distorted Perception

hung their heads as they made their way out. Allison fixed the lock on the outside of the door and Kathleen watched them walk down the driveway. She was devastated and embarrassed that they could live like this, they had gone through it themselves, and they still didn't tell her.

All at once it hit her and she dropped down to the floor. Maxwell had told her that Allison was his sister. She was not his sister. She was his first victim.

Each woman came in turn with Allison to try to talk to Kathleen and assure her that this lifestyle was what they all wanted. Janie was the one that Kathleen wanted to speak to. But she wanted to talk to her when Allison wasn't around. Janie was the one who seemed to be the sweetest and Kathleen had no doubt she was the one who had been hit the hardest by the news. She wanted to know how she dealt with it. What was it that made Janie change her mind about wanting to stay here? Allison wouldn't leave them alone for even a moment. As they were leaving, Kathleen grabbed Janie by the arm and whispered, "I want to talk to you alone." Janie just nodded and followed Allison out the door.

Three hours later she came back and knocked on the window. They had to practically scream at each other in order to hear. Janie told her not to worry too much. Maxwell would let her out soon and as soon as he did, Kathleen should make her way to Janie's house where they would be able to talk properly. Kathleen was thankful that she was willing to speak to her about it and she felt much better overall because of it. There was no way she was going to keep going the way she had been. She needed to get out of the house as soon as she could before she started going crazy.

At the end of the week, Maxwell came home and finally took the lock off the door. Kathleen guessed he had spoken with the other women, and they assured him that she wasn't going to try to go anywhere. The first day she was free to leave her house, she headed over to Janie's as she said she would. She had spent days thinking about both sides, wondering what she would do if Maxwell brought home another woman. Would feeling his anger be worth trying to warn someone else? Would it do any good to warn them knowing they couldn't leave even if they wanted to? She was excited to see Janie and hoped she might be able to help her through her thoughts.

They hadn't gotten any more snow since the first storm, but it was still bitter cold outside. Kathleen's feet and hands were numb by the time she got next door.

Janie had seen her leave her house and immediately put on some coffee so she could warm up. She stepped outside once earlier in the morning and the temperature was well below what her body could tolerate. She watched Kathleen make her way down the road and thought for a moment that she could see her belly starting to fill out a bit. It was hard to tell under her jacket and sweater. Janie knew what she was going through but she was still excited about the baby and about not having to hide the truth from her anymore. She felt awful about not being able to say anything and it had been eating her up. She really liked Kathleen and wanted nothing more than to be honest with her.

Janie opened the door as Kathleen walked up the front steps and stepped aside to let her in. "You look cold."

Her teeth were chattering as she answered. "It is so cold out there. And that wind is terrible. It goes right through you. Speaking of..." She took off her jacket and hung it on the hook inside the door before making her way down the hall to the bathroom. When she got back, Janie had some coffee on the table for her.

"Don't worry. It's decaf." She shot her a smile and then dove right into her speech. "I know you're mad. I don't blame you. It took me a long time to come to terms with what was happening, too. But honey, it really is amazing here and I hope you'll be able to forgive me with time. Please understand we all wanted to tell you, we wanted to protect you. It makes us all uncomfortable at first, but we need to protect ourselves too. You do understand that don't you?" She looked at her with pity in her eyes.

Kathleen knew she was referring to the blow she took to the head. She touched the side of her face with the tips of her fingers and almost perfectly traced where the edges of the bruise had been. Even though the swelling had gone down, and the colors were fading, she thought she may always feel it there. She nodded her head to indicate that she did understand what Janie was trying to tell her. And she felt awful that the others had to go through exactly what she feared. "I just felt so betrayed by all of you, Janie. Knowing that you've all been through it yourselves. I feel as though someone should have said something.

But at the same time, I guess, maybe I wouldn't have said anything either knowing what may come from it. It's just all so confusing. I don't understand how all of this could have happened right under my nose and I had no idea that it was going on."

Janie nodded. "We all went through it. We know. And each of us also said that we would help the next person that came in. But when it came time, we just couldn't do it. We've seen what happens and it's not worth the risk. Kathleen, I'm sorry. I really am."

Kathleen stood and wrapped her arms around Janie. "I forgive you. It's just hard, you know?"

"For all of us, Honey. It's hard for all of us."

She gently eased herself from Janie's embrace. "Can I ask a question?"

"Of course. Everything is in the open now. We can answer all your questions."

Kathleen just stared at her for a moment. "Allison?" She raised her eyebrows and curled up her lip hoping that Janie would know what she was asking.

"Not his sister. Allison is Maxwell's first wife. He trusts her now, but it took a long time. She's been through more than any of us." She closed her eyes and shook her head. "I was so angry with her when I went through what you're struggling with now. But then I realized what she had gone through. She was the first. Could you imagine how she felt when Maxwell just brought another woman home? He didn't even try to hide it from her like a normal person would if they were having an affair. The way I understand it, they moved out here and within six months he moved Rebecca in across the street and basically told Allison outright 'She's my new wife. Behave or she'll replace you completely.' Needless to say, Allison and Rebecca didn't speak to each other for quite some time. They held what Maxwell was doing against each other instead of against him. If Maxwell spent the night at Rebecca's, Allison was mad at Rebecca. And Rebecca felt the same way when it was reversed. It wasn't until I showed up that they started speaking and realized it was Maxwell they should be mad at. After I found out about the other two, we tried to revolt against him. That was a big mistake. All three of us walked around with matching bruises for weeks. Before we stood up to him, we all used to secretly hope that he would decide to come spend the night with us. It was a power trip if you will. But after we stood up to him it was a completely different story. Two of us were pregnant at the time and we hoped and prayed that he would choose any house except our own. He was angry and as you know, he took it out on us. He needed the power and the control, and he took it any way he could."

"Any way that he could? What do you mean by that?"

"He knew we were all terrified. He enjoyed knowing that we were afraid of him coming to our homes. A few times, he thought he was being funny, and he would drive his truck into the driveway, get out and start walking toward the door and then get back in his truck and leave. He knew we were all sitting in our windows watching for him to come home. So, when two of us saw him pull into someone else's driveway we were relieved, and the third person was terrified. And then it flipped us all around when he backed out of the driveway again. I can't tell you how anxious that made all of us. We didn't know what was happening in other homes because he locked us all in unless he was physically there with us. He starved Rebecca when she was pregnant with her first. He left her with little food to begin with and then didn't bring her any for over two weeks. She wasn't afraid for herself. She was afraid for her baby. That was the ultimate power for Maxwell."

Kathleen had tears crawling silently down her cheeks. She hung her head and could feel her muscles tiring as if she were having an anxiety attack. It didn't take long for her to become protective of her unborn child and she couldn't wrap her mind around what Rebecca must have been feeling. She curled her arms around her own stomach in a protective manner. "How did Allison gain his trust?" She had to reason that if one of them was able to, maybe she could as well.

"I know what you're thinking. We've all tried. But as long as Allison is around, none of us will gain that level of trust from him. With that being said, Allison gained his trust by betraying someone else. They had confided in her that they were planning to leave. She ran back and told him." Janie raised a hand to stop Kathleen from interrupting. "I know what you're thinking again. And yes, we forgave her for it. She felt awful about it because she was ostracized from all of us for months. We were supposed to be a team and she betrayed us all. None of us were willing to speak to her. Obviously, we forgave her. She hasn't done anything like that since. But that was all Maxwell needed to know he could trust her completely. And not one of us is dumb enough to try to leave anyway. You said it yourself. We have absolutely nowhere to go. We'd probably starve or freeze or dehydrate before we got anywhere near a town."

Kathleen changed the subject completely. "What about the doctor? Hasn't anyone tried to say anything to him? Tell him that we're being held against our will?"

Janie couldn't help but laugh. "That's the part you may struggle with understanding for a while to come. We don't feel like we're being held here anymore. Those of us that were here before you like it here. We are not going anywhere. And before you get any cute ideas, just don't. Maxwell will be there, right by your side, every time Dr. Caldwell is with you. He won't leave you alone with him for a moment."

"Huh." It was all Kathleen could think of to say. She thought she had all the conversation she would be able to have for the day. She thanked Janie for the information and coffee and trudged her way back home.

She spent the next three hours sitting at her kitchen table trying to process all the information she had gained from Janie. The hardest thing for her was when she figured out that Cayden was not Maxwell's nephew, but his son. It hit her all at once. He was the oldest son and by default that meant Maxwell was teaching him to lie and cheat in the same way he did. He was grooming him to do the exact same thing whether Cayden realized it yet or not. Kathleen wondered if Allison knew.

Allison...she was with Maxwell the night that he ran into Vicki. Her best friend had been right all along.

When Maxwell came home from work that night he went straight to Allison's house. He needed to find out what Kathleen had done throughout her day. He knew full well that wherever she went, that person would have turned around and told Allison everything they had talked about. He was surprised to hear that she wasn't as inquisitive, comparatively speaking, as the others. She either was just as naive as Maxwell had thought or he really could trust her not to try to go anywhere. He figured he would find out when he stopped by her house the next day. He was too tired to speak to her today. He had brought Cayden out with him again that morning and this time, he didn't have to wait for a phone call. Rosemary accepted his invitation for a date with great enthusiasm. This time, he aimed high, and set out to find someone with a nursing degree so he wouldn't have to bother the doctor with every little thing. So far, he was feeling good about it.

Chapter XV

Five months later Kathleen was busying herself setting up a school room for the children. The old barn sat on the far edge of the property Maxwell owned. There was a barely visible path leading up to the doorway, a clear sign the barn and land surrounding had not been maintained for a number of years. Brown, brittle weeds grew nearly half-way up the outside of the structure. Inside, the wooden floors were covered in a heavy layer of dirt and the walls were coated with thick spider webs. The late summer sun streamed in through cracks in the walls and the roof. Old, discarded tables, desks, and mismatched chairs were stacked haphazardly along the room's outer edges. With all the women pitching in, it took three days for the room to be cleared of filth and set up in an orderly fashion.

Kathleen had set up a schooling plan and discussed her ideas with the other women. With only a few minor changes and suggestions, they all agreed to the curriculum she came up with. Kathleen's previous experience as a teacher stopped the others from questioning her plan.

Allison convinced Maxwell to purchase paper, pens, pencils, and some books. She even got him to find a used, stand-alone chalkboard so Kathleen had something to write on. Nametags were placed in front of each chair along with a pad of paper, two pencils, a pen, and a book. The nametags and books were placed strategically to keep the children seated according to their age group. Without knowing the exact reading level of any of the kids, Kathleen requested specific books and hoped she was close with her guess. She looked around the room and was pleased with how well it all came together. They didn't have much by way of classroom décor, so the women all wrote signs with inspirational quotes on them and crudely displayed them around the room.

Kathleen was finding it harder to get around. She felt like her belly was growing daily and she was tiring more easily. She was thankful the women all had a hand in helping her. As the months had gone by, she realized what they were all trying to tell her from the beginning. They were a family. They all helped each other with anything that needed to be done. Within their six households, Kathleen felt more love than she had ever felt in her life. She loved all the children and the women. It was the best family she could ask for and she was getting more excited, as the days went on, to add her own little one to the mix.

She had two days left until the date Maxwell had set for the beginning of the school year. She was finishing up some lesson plans and began to worry about teaching different age groups at the same time. She had no idea what the kids had been taught so far and without wanting to insult anyone, she was preparing for the worst. She planned to spend the first week testing the children to see where she needed to start with each of them. It was making planning ahead difficult, but she knew she would be starting with the basics with the younger kids so that's where she focused her efforts. It had been a long time since she taught children so young.

Janie came by the schoolroom and brought her a sandwich for lunch. Kathleen had asked her to be a teacher's aide and provide support to the younger children while she focused on the older ones. She had never taught multiple subjects or age ranges at the same time and she was feeling overwhelmed by the idea. Samantha had agreed to make lunches for all the kids for the first week and would bring them by the makeshift schoolhouse just around noon. Megan and Rebecca were combining efforts to make dinner on the days that the kids were in school. Allison didn't fully commit to anything directly related to the schooling but offered to help wherever she was needed and would watch any children that were below the schooling age. Kathleen couldn't believe how easy it was to get everyone to take a role. Even when she worked for the public school system, she could never find anyone to help her out for more than an hour or two.

The first week went much smoother than Kathleen anticipated, the children all seemed to enjoy learning. She was taken aback by the lack of knowledge of the older kids. Samantha had told her everyone educated their children. At the time, Kathleen didn't find it necessary to ask any further questions. But after spending a full week assessing their knowledge, she knew it was going to be quite a bit of work to get them where they needed to be. Still, she was looking forward to beginning the lessons and watching the children take pride in their understanding of math and English.

During the second week, Janie confided in her that she was exhausted. "I had no idea being an aide would be so much work. How are you able to manage all this and still walk out at the end of the day with a smile on your face?"

Kathleen knew Janie was trying her best but, despite her chipper personality, she got frustrated easily when she felt like a child was purposely being difficult. Kathleen laughed. "They're kids. If they don't feel like doing something, they're going to tell you they can't. And then they'll get frustrated with you when you try to show them how. It happens all the time and there isn't much you can do to fix that. But you can't let it get to you. Just keep doing what you're doing, the kids will come around."

Janie didn't believe her for a moment but she humored her and nodded her head. It was only week two and she wanted to pull her hair out. "We may need to renegotiate my contract."

"Fine," Kathleen replied. "As part of your new contract, I'll let you help me clean the chalkboard." She held an eraser out to Janie and stuck her tongue out at her before walking away.

"You're such a child."

"Uh oh. Are you going to get frustrated with me, too?"

Janie hurled the eraser in Kathleen's direction and left a perfect white rectangle on the arm of her black blouse. Kathleen felt like she was back in school again and she loved it. She hadn't realized until that moment that she was finally happy again, the classroom is where she was meant to be. She smiled at

Janie. "Let's get this done so we can relax before dinner."

Maxwell had taken to spending one night at each house and leaving for three or four days at a time. Kathleen was the only one who was bothered by it. She tried asking Megan about it but was met with a strong resistance to answer the question. Megan told her not to ask because she didn't want to know. Kathleen took that as a hint to leave it alone, but it still bothered her.

When she didn't know about the others, she assumed he was out working. Once she learned the truth, she figured he was staying with one of them for the evening. Now, she knew he was out of town and had no idea where he was, or who he was with. Was he really out of town for work or was he out looking for his next unsuspecting victim? The thought made Kathleen sick to her stomach. She didn't think she would be able to be as strong as the others. She felt like if he brought someone else home, she would blurt it out the moment she met her. She tried to put her mind at ease and convince herself that it would be a long time before she had to worry about something like that. She was wrong.

Less than a month later, Maxwell was opening the house that sat by itself on the corner of the road. All the women seemed to be in shock. This was the quickest turnaround they had ever witnessed. None of them were happy about it. They nominated Allison to be their speaker of the house and she went to confront Maxwell about his intentions.

She was gone for less than an hour and upon her return she repeated, verbatim, what Maxwell had told her. No one mentioned it but they could all see a handprint clearly outlined on her face. Allison had pulled her hair forward in an attempt to hide it but she was failing miserably. "Maxwell says it's still going to be a while. Right now, he's concerned mostly about being there for Kathleen and her baby. He has some fixing up to do on the vacant house, so he wanted to open it up sooner than he usually does." The look on her face matched everyone else's.

It was confirmed. He was bringing home another woman within a year of Kathleen moving in. None of them knew what to make of it. It was usually at least two years before he was brave enough to bring another person in. He either had something up his sleeve or he was moving too fast and he was going to slip up and something would go terribly wrong again.

Kathleen was due any day and the doctor had been to see her more regularly. All the women were treating her like a delicate flower, not allowing her to do anything herself. Knowing how difficult it was to give birth outside a hospital, they wanted to keep her level of stress as low as possible. They didn't have to worry about it for long. Kathleen's stomach began cramping around lunchtime and it had gotten worse as the hours went on. At two-thirty the following morning, she stumbled down the street to Janie's house. The closer she got, the farther away it felt. Twice, she stopped and dropped to her knees, waiting for the pain to subside.

When Janie opened the door, she found Kathleen doubled over in pain. She ran outside, placing her arm around her shoulder and helped her into the house. After she was safely laying on the couch, Janie shoved her feet into her boots and ran down the road to Megan's house to get Maxwell. It took all three of them to get Kathleen back to her own house before Maxwell set out to get the doctor.

By seven in the morning, Abigail Sophia Lewis had arrived. Kathleen was exhausted after being awake all night and fighting the pains of labor. She cried for almost two hours straight while she held Abigail in her arms. She had never known a love so pure until she looked into her baby's face. Abigail's innocent wails pulled at her heart in a way she never thought would be possible. She already couldn't imagine life without her.

Throughout the day, the women took turns stopping by Kathleen's house to make sure she was okay. Earlier in the week, they had brought over one of the bassinets they had been swapping between each other for years, glad to see it in use again. They knew Kathleen and Abigail would most likely be sleeping. They also knew Maxwell would be of no help if she did need something. Maxwell left the house only long enough to grab dinner at another house and then he went back to Kathleen's. He was not taking care of her, he was not caring for Abigail, he was just in the house, somehow believing that was enough. The women had all gotten used to that and they each took shifts going over to the house, including the hours overnight. Maxwell slept on the couch to allow them all to tend to Kathleen and the baby. Although it was Kathleen's first experience with it, Maxwell had made it clear to the other women that he wanted no part of taking care of an infant. None of them understood since he was the one who wanted so many children, but as they always do, they banded together to help each other so when it was their turn again, they would have help as well.

Maxwell hadn't paid any attention to Abigail. As time wore on, he spent less time at Kathleen's house and when he did come home, he all but ignored the baby. It wasn't until she was three months old that he picked her up for the first time. Abigail screamed and wailed but he held her as though she were sleeping.

Kathleen was so pleased that he finally seemed to be taking a liking to her, it made her eyes well up with tears. Seeing him hold their child was exactly what she imagined it being like from the beginning, before all of the insanity of the past year. She couldn't help it; she walked up and wrapped her arms around both of them and wept on Maxwell's shoulder. "I do love you, you know," she whispered.

"I know you do."

Chapter XVI

Abigail had just turned five months old when she began getting sick. She was feverish and fussy. She was throwing up her milk, her face was flushed. Kathleen made Maxwell have the doctor come out three times in one week. She seemed to be getting worse even while taking the medicine the doctor had given to Kathleen. During his third visit Kathleen begged him to take Abigail to a hospital so she could get the care she needed. Dr. Caldwell hung his head. His eyes were closed, he was shaking his head. "In my professional opinion, she won't survive the trip." He turned his back on Kathleen and whispered to Maxwell. "I would make arrangements." Kathleen burst into tears and hugged her daughter tight.

Allison ran into the doctor in the driveway and spoke to him for a moment. She knew he wouldn't say anything to her but she knew him well enough to be able to read his reaction. She asked him only three questions and got all the answers she needed without him saying a word. She let herself inside and walked straight past Kathleen who was sobbing uncontrollably over the baby in her arms. She grabbed Maxwell by his arm and pulled him out the back door.

She had no concern over what that would mean for her later in the day. It would be worth it.

"You did it, didn't you?" She hissed. Her muscles were tense and her hands were clenched as tight as she could get them. She knew just by his facial expression that she was right. "What the fuck, Maxwell?!" She started to raise her voice without caring that the sound carried outside. "She's only an infant... your infant. What on earth would possess you to do such a thing?" She yelled through clenched teeth, worried that if she relaxed her jaw, her angry energy would transfer and she would punch Maxwell in the face. She waited for him to speak but he stared over her shoulder, across the field. She quieted her voice. "Is it too late?"

He nodded his head once. "I have never hated you more than I do at this moment." Allison reached over and slapped him across the face as hard as she could. Her hand stung and the sound of the impact echoed off the side of the house. "Whatever is coming to me...that was worth it." She pushed by him, ripped the door open, and slammed it behind her.

She approached Kathleen and kissed the top of her head. "I love you, Honey." She stroked Abigail's cheek with the backs of her fingers and walked out the front door. By the time she got home, her face was streaked with tears. As soon as she closed her door, she leaned her back against it and slid down to the floor. She couldn't stop the constant flow of tears from coming. Her youngest daughter came into the room and sat on the floor next to her wrapping her arms around her. Allison grabbed her and pulled her close. She felt so helpless. She couldn't imagine what she would do if she didn't have any one of her children.

She held her daughter until she fell asleep and Allison carried her off to bed. She entered each bedroom and hugged and kissed each one of her children. She had never been so thankful to have them in her life. She went to the kitchen to make herself a cup of tea. She didn't believe she would sleep a wink that night.

She did sleep. Allison fell asleep at the kitchen table and was woken by a pounding on her front door. She forgot she had locked the door last night in her state of confusion and hurt. She wanted warning in case Maxwell decided to show up. Her eyes were burning and she knew they were puffy and red from crying. She barely turned the lock before the door flew open and Megan fell into her arms. Allison didn't need to ask. She wrapped her arms around her and held her tight. The two cried on the other's shoulder and only let go when one of the kids interrupted.

"Are you okay, mommy?" Allison's youngest son looked up at her with his big brown eyes and she laughed at how innocent he looked. It was all nerves, she knew, but it made her feel better to smile and she knew it was better for him to see that.

"We're okay, baby. We just got some bad news that upset us a little bit but we're all better now. Do you want some breakfast? I'll get out some bowls if you go wake up your sisters and brother." She smiled at him again and patted him on the butt when he turned away screaming for his siblings. She heard the thumping of his bare feet as he ran through the hallway and she broke down in tears again.

Megan did the same but put her hand on Allison's back and guided her to the kitchen. "Let's get your kids fed and then we'll figure out what to do."

Allison pulled bowls and spoons out while Megan grabbed cereal boxes and milk. "How did you find out?"

Megan took a few deep breaths before she could answer. I went over to check on Kathleen this morning. I knocked, you know, because Maxwell is there. He opened the door with a blank expression on his face. He just shook his head at me and closed the door in my face. He didn't say anything. He didn't have to. I knew in my heart. There's just no way you can mistake that feeling."

Allison nodded. "The others?"

"I came straight here."

"This is going to be a rough day."

While the children ate, Allison and Megan spoke in the living room about what they were going to do. They agreed the best thing would be to gather all the women and go to Kathleen's house as a group. There was no way Maxwell would be able to deny them all. They left instructions for Allison's children to get dressed and go over to Janie's house. The two of them set off to deliver the news. They decided to start at the far end and work their way back, pitching in where needed to get all the kids fed and clothed.

When they reached the end of her driveway, they saw Samantha poke her head out her front door. She saw the look on both their faces and didn't need to ask. Her eyes dropped and her shoulders fell. "Come in. I'll get the kids." Maybe they wouldn't have to tell anyone after all. Allison guessed everyone knew how bad the situation was but no one wanted to discuss it for fear of it coming true. She felt so alone knowing what she knew. She wished she could spill all the information so she wouldn't have to carry the burden alone.

Neither Megan nor Allison said a word to anyone. They all knew how much Kathleen must be hurting, some understood more deeply than others. They also knew Maxwell would be offering zero support to her. Allison was the only one aware of exactly how insensitive he would be to the situation.

While they were walking, Allison thought about all the other tragedies that had fallen upon them over the years and began to wonder if they really were accidents and natural deaths or if something worse was happening. She knew it was probably unfair to think such things but given what she knew about Abigail, she thought her doubts were justified.

By the time they reached Janie's house, she was standing on the porch. It was hard to miss that many people heading in her direction. Her heart started racing and she wanted to scream and cry. "The kids are in the back yard. Head on back." The whole group of children ran around the side of the house and the women walked somberly up to the porch. Janie motioned with her arm to direct them inside. "I'm guessing I already know the news. Has anyone seen Kathleen yet?"

They all shook their heads. Megan was the only one to speak. Her voice broke and got caught in her throat when she started. "No. I tried to go over this morning and Maxwell closed the door on me. The look on his face told me all I needed to know." She took a deep breath. "Allison and I thought it would be best if we all went over together. Kathleen needs the love and support right now and I think we all know that Maxwell is not exactly the consoling type."

Pieces of conversation got all jumbled together as they all spoke at once.

"I agree."

"We should be there with her."

"We understand what she's going through, he doesn't."

"He's never cared about any of the babies."

"We should go as a group."

Allison was relieved they all felt the same way. Together they left Janie's house and headed over to Kathleen's. Maxwell must have heard them coming because he opened the door before they had the chance to break it down. "Megan. I already told you no." His figure loomed in the doorway and created a barricade to the house.

"Maxwell, she needs us right now. You don't understand what she's going through. Please, let us see her. If she doesn't want us here, let her tell us and we'll go. Please?"

Maxwell started to resist but Kathleen appeared in the doorway wrapped in a blanket. She reached out and touched his shoulder. "It's okay. They can come in. I think we were all expecting it." She sounded terrible and looked even worse. When Maxwell stepped to the side, they could see her, arms wrapped around herself, puffy eyes, red nose. It looked as though she hadn't slept for weeks. "Besides, it'll give you a chance to see if you can get the doctor." He stepped back from the door to let them all inside. He grunted and pulled his keys from his pocket before walking out the door.

Allison had to stop herself from purposely tripping him down the stairs. She couldn't even look at his face, although she desperately wanted to see if she had left a mark on it. At the thought, she could feel the tingle growing in her hand again and she got a sick sense of satisfaction from it. She pleaded with herself to stop thinking that way, knowing he probably felt the same way every time he did it to one of them. She told herself to stop thinking about it and focus on Kathleen. She was why they were here.

She walked into the kitchen to make some coffee for everyone. She needed a few minutes to clear her head before she went and joined the rest of them. After she turned the coffee pot on, Allison sat at the table for a moment. She couldn't believe Maxwell had waited all this time to go get the doctor. It had been well over an hour since Megan came crying at her door. They had no idea what time it happened. But it also meant that the baby was still here and all she could imagine was its lifeless, tiny body lying in the bassinet that all their children had once laid in. Her eyes welled up again and she physically shook her head to try to get the image out. She had to keep it together for now. She could cry all she wanted once she got back home. She brought out the first round of coffee and went back into the kitchen to make a second pot for the rest. Rebecca followed her.

"I didn't know if you wanted any help. But I thought you should know, I'm a little concerned about Kathleen. She's not acting at all like I expected her to. I know she may just be in shock, but it doesn't seem to be bothering her at all." She pulled out a chair and sat down. "Plus, I needed to get away for a minute. You can tell she had been crying earlier but she's so calm now, I almost feel the need to break down for her. I know exactly how she feels but I don't remember ever acting like that."

Allison wasn't sure how to respond. If Rebecca only knew half of what she did. She walked around the table and rubbed her back for a minute to try to console her. "I think it is just shock but we'll keep an eye on her over the next couple of days to make sure she's progressing the way she should through the grief process."

Rebecca nodded and stood. She grabbed two coffee mugs before heading back out to join everyone in the living room. Allison stayed in the kitchen a few minutes more to make sure that she could handle facing everyone without completely breaking down. She took a few deep breaths and blew them out slowly. She joined them on the couches and did her best to concentrate on the conversation but kept finding herself fading away from it.

The following three days were somber. Between the five women, they made a visitation plan so each of them would check up on Kathleen a few times a day. They made sure she was doing okay mentally and eating and drinking. As they all expected, Maxwell was less than consoling and he made all of them uncomfortable with how far removed he was from any sort of feelings over his child's death. He seemed more annoyed by the fact that everyone else seemed to care so much.

Maxwell had employed the older boys to dig a small grave on the edge of the yard, away from the house. Kathleen had begged him to keep Abigail close so she could visit her at any time.

On the fourth day, they all dressed in funeral attire and met in Kathleen's backyard. The day was cold and heavy raindrops were falling in spurts causing the scent of the freshly turned earth to circle around them. They had a small ceremony celebrating Abigail's life and the few months they got to spend with her on Earth. It was much shorter than Kathleen expected it to be. She was grateful, as she wanted it over. She wanted everyone to leave so she could say goodbye to her sweet child alone. She spent the entire service staring, through watery eyes, into the empty hole. She didn't allow herself to cry, she couldn't hear the words that were being shared. She just kept imagining Abigail laying on the dirt, alone, crying, and pleading to be picked up and comforted. She refused to accept that her baby, her angel, would soon occupy that void in the earth. When the service was over, Kathleen didn't stand there to converse with anyone. She made her way back to her house alone.

Everyone was expected at Rebecca's house for a lunch following the service. They all made their way down in their own time. Samantha was the first to notice that neither Kathleen nor Maxwell were there. When she looked down the street she saw no sign of Maxwell's truck. She whispered to Allison that she was going to check on Kathleen and slipped out the front door.

When she got to the house, she knocked lightly before opening the door and walking in. "Kathleen? Are you here?" She didn't see her in the living room or the kitchen. The house felt hollow. It was eerily quiet except for the echo of her footsteps. "Kathleen? We're worried about you. I just came to see how you were doing." She started walking down the hallway and thought she could hear a whispered voice coming from one of the rooms. The door to the master bedroom was open a bit. Samantha pushed it open a little more and the hinges groaned in protest. She poked her head in. "Kathleen?"

She gasped and covered her mouth with her hand. She found her crouched in a corner cradling the small, wooden casket in her arms. Her cheek was resting on the rough, slatted surface and she was lightly stroking the side of the box. Tears rolled silently down her face as she choked out the words to 'Hush, Little Baby'. If she heard Samantha come in, she didn't let on. She continued swaying in time to her words as if to rock Abigail to sleep.

Samantha's stomach clenched and the muscles in her throat tensed up. She thought she might find Kathleen crying, curled up in her bed, but she wasn't prepared for this. She had no idea what to do. She wanted to run over and hug her and tell her everything would be okay, but she couldn't. She stayed motionless and watched Kathleen for a full minute before she turned and bolted out of the house. Whatever needed to be done, she knew she couldn't do it on her own.

In one motion, she ran through Rebecca's front door, grabbed the arms of both Allison and Janie and ran out the back door pulling them both with her. Neither one asked any questions, they just followed where Samantha led them. When they entered Kathleen's house, she turned to them and raised her finger to her lips and pointed towards the bedroom. They both walked slowly down the hall and peered through the opening of the door. Allison took a step back when she realized what she was seeing. Janie gasped and ran into the bedroom.

Samantha could only hear the murmur of voices coming from the bedroom but couldn't bring herself to go back in. Allison remained in place in the hallway. She had never seen anything like it. It scared her. She felt as though she were watching a disturbing, morbid scene from a horror movie and couldn't quite distinguish reality from fantasy at that moment. She heard Janie speaking but couldn't make sense of the words.

After a few minutes Janie emerged holding the casket in her arms. "I...I don't...I'm going to set this on the back porch for now." She squeezed between them as she made her way through the hall. The sight of Janie brought both Allison and Samantha back to the present. They could hear Kathleen sobbing and they glanced at each other. Neither one wanted to take the lead but they both knew they had to go in and see her. They made their way into the bedroom together. Kathleen was still curled up on the floor. She had her knees hugged to her chest and her face was buried. They knelt on either side of her and lowered their heads to her shoulders.

It was two months before Kathleen began to act like her old self again. She had missed all but the first two months of the school year but Janie had stepped up in hopes of continuing what Kathleen had started with the kids. Megan replaced Janie as the aide and Allison took over making lunch for everyone. Samantha and Rebecca still alternated dinners for everyone. When the school year ended, Janie felt good about what they had been able to accomplish. She was still getting frustrated easily but she found it easier teaching an entire room of children than she did teaching just her own kids.

Less than a week after the funeral, Maxwell brought his new wife home. The women all did their best to act as the friendly neighbor they always played, but it was much more difficult given the circumstances this time around. Everyone was livid with Maxwell for bringing her home at such a time and practically throwing Kathleen to the side. He had only visited her about twice a month and had no communication with her when he was there. He showed up, ate his dinner, took what he needed from her, and left again. He hadn't been to see Allison once since Abigail died.

     Kathleen woke up one day at the end of June and she was shocked. She felt refreshed and alive. She made herself some coffee, showered, and dressed. She had a renewed feeling that she could conquer the world. Until now, she had only seen Maxwell's new wife from a distance and she decided she should finally go and introduce herself. It had been too much for her to handle with losing her child and trying to act like a friendly neighbor to a woman she both felt bad for and despised at the same time. She hadn't been able to bring herself to speak to her or meet her in any capacity. The others understood and made sure to keep them separate as much as they could.

     Maxwell's new wife was named Rosemary. Although she was younger than Kathleen, she had more of a grandmotherly quality to her. She was heavy set and her hair was always pulled back in a bun. Kathleen learned, through their brief conversation, she didn't have any children yet but was anxiously waiting for it to happen. She had been a nurse before Maxwell had suggested they move out to the country. Rosemary told Kathleen she thought it was a wonderful idea as she was looking forward to a fresh start and a wholesome place to raise her potential children.

Kathleen liked how sweet she was but also thought she was full of it. She knew exactly why Rosemary wanted to move out here. She had been through it all herself. She believed that she and Maxwell would grow closer again if they moved away from so many people. Kathleen was confident in her assessment and pulled most of that confidence from the sight of the healing bruise on Rosemary's cheek. Like everyone else, she had tried to cover it but ultimately failed.

On her walk home, Kathleen was struggling with her feelings toward Rosemary. She despised her for the first few weeks because she was Maxwell's new wife. She knew it wasn't fair. Rosemary didn't do it on purpose, she didn't know any better than Kathleen did when she got married. Rosemary would be just as shocked as the rest of them when she found out what was happening. In her head, Kathleen was accusing her of lying, even though she did the exact same thing when she first got here. She was also fighting her own feelings over her promise to herself that she would tell the next woman who arrived. She didn't tell Rosemary. She was trying to justify it by blaming her emotional state, but she knew it wasn't valid. She didn't tell her because she couldn't. She was afraid to say anything, just like she imagined all the others were.

In early August, both Kathleen and Rosemary broke the news that they were pregnant. It sent Kathleen into a downward spiral for a few weeks, feeling like she had somehow betrayed Abigail. But the excitement eventually won out. This year she knew the timing would make it so she would be able to spend all but maybe the last month schooling the children, which was much better than the previous year. She was still so grateful that Janie had taken over in her absence and for having no formal training she had done a great job keeping them all on schedule. She hoped she would volunteer to do the same at the end of this school year.

Over the summer, Maxwell had begun taking the older boys out with him more often. None of the boys would talk about it but the women all thought it was nice to finally see him spending time with his kids. He all but ignored them when he was home and the girls still didn't get as much as a hello from him, but at least he was taking some interest in some of the kids. It surprised Kathleen when she learned that Maxwell's main goal was to have as many children as he could. She had to question why when he never felt the need to spend any time with them. She didn't even know for sure if he knew all their names.

He seemed to be overly pleased with himself that he had two wives that were expecting a child within days of each other again. It made Kathleen feel a bit sick to her stomach when she thought about it that way but she was getting used to the idea that he was at a different house every night. She had been there over a year and a half and it simply became a way of life for her as much as she hated the thought of it. Kathleen believed Rosemary was even more naïve than she was. She never questioned how Kathleen became pregnant, she was just excited to share her pregnancy enjoyment with someone else she had grown to like.

There had been snippets of conversation about Maxwell and how it wasn't smart on his part, considering Rosemary had not yet questioned anything about the living arrangements to anyone. She was the happy-go-lucky type and seemed content to be around people that she could converse with. They all dreaded the day she began to ask questions.

Depending on the day, Kathleen wanted to grab her by the shoulders and shake her. Tell her to wake up and look at her surroundings. She had to at least have an inkling that something about this picture wasn't right. But she just kept carrying on about what she might want to name the baby and how happy she was that her child would have a trained professional for a teacher. That was her main concern when Maxwell mentioned moving so far out to the country. Once he told her he had a teacher and a school she was all in. She couldn't wait to move away from the city.

Chapter XVII

Both babies were born at the beginning of May. To everyone's surprise, Maxwell was overjoyed. He had two new boys. He didn't show much affection toward the babies but his attitude toward all the women changed significantly. They wanted to keep it that way as long as possible. On the last day of school for the year, Kathleen decided to take her baby to the schoolhouse to show all the kids. To her surprise, Rosemary had the same idea. Kathleen saw her standing in the back of the classroom with the baby carrier at her feet.

They had visited each other a few times over the past few weeks as a way of maintaining their sanity. They got along well enough, but Kathleen knew she would never be as close to Rosemary as she was to Janie or Megan. There was something about her that she couldn't quite place, she didn't trust her as much as she did the others. They hugged and Kathleen took a seat away from her in the back of the room until Janie was done teaching for the day. She was just about to get up to bring her son to the front of the classroom when she felt Rosemary staring at her. She turned to look at her and saw nothing but rage on her face. Kathleen was taken aback but mouthed the words, "What's the matter?"

Rosemary stood up from where she had taken a seat, her body rigid as she approached Kathleen. She whispered as loud as she could, "Where did your baby come from?"

Kathleen let out a noise that sounded like a snort causing everyone to turn and to see what was happening. "Excuse me?"

Rosemary glared at her. "You heard me. None of us ever leave and the only male besides Maxwell that I've ever seen here is the doctor. So, where did your baby come from?" Her voice was stern and a little intimidating to Kathleen as she had come to think of her as having such a gentle demeanor.

She had yet to be briefed on how to appropriately answer any questions that arose, so she fell back on her defenses. "I don't like your tone of voice. If you'd like to talk to me, I would change your attitude first." She got up, grabbed the baby's carrier, and headed to the front of the classroom. She pulled Janie aside in the middle of a sentence to warn her and then took her leave.

Instead of going home like she had planned, she went straight to Allison's house to tell her that Rosemary was asking questions.

Allison laughed nervously. "Well, it was bound to happen eventually. It took her a long time, though." She hoisted herself up to sit on the kitchen counter. "I don't mean to be insensitive, but it is a little bit funny that she's trying to blame you." She shook her head. "We all thought it was a really bad move on Maxwell's part to get her pregnant at the same time as you since she didn't know yet. He got lucky with how long it took her to figure it out."

Kathleen didn't think it was funny at all. She wasn't mad at Rosemary. She understood where her frustration came from. She was mad at Maxwell for doing this to another unsuspecting woman.

"Why don't you head on home. I'll go over to the school to see if I can help Janie out."

She took Allison's advice and went back to her house. She was worried about how mad Rosemary was and hoped she would calm down before she talked to Maxwell. Kathleen knew what it was like to be in her position. It wasn't that long ago that she felt the same level of confusion and betrayal. She hoped Rosemary was smart enough not to go after Maxwell with the same attitude she came after her with. She was also worried about herself. If Rosemary didn't ask about it the right way, Maxwell may try to blame Kathleen as well. Physically, she didn't think she would be able to handle that right now.

As was customary, Allison met Maxwell when he returned home to tell him about Rosemary. He had only been to see Allison a few times in the past couple months, not as often as she was used to. Like Allison, Maxwell laughed when she told him. "About damn time. I was beginning to worry about her competency."

Allison just glared at him. She was surprised as well, but she didn't think his comment was appropriate. "That's not funny, Maxwell."

"No, it's not. There was a fifty-fifty chance she would have passed that gene onto the kid."

Allison rolled her eyes and sighed. "Anyway, you should probably go see her tonight because she's trying to blame Kathleen. We really don't need that around here."

"Fine." He turned his truck around, leaving Allison standing in a cloud of dust.

Samantha heard yelling and loud noises throughout the evening but didn't put much thought into it. These were frequent occurrences here, and they happened to all of them. They all knew to give each other space. The following morning, Maxwell stopped by her house before he left for work. He had the baby with him and when Samantha greeted him, he shoved the carrier at her. "You need to watch him for a few days."

Samantha's eyes widened and she grabbed for the carrier, worried that he may drop it at her feet. "Is everything okay?"

"Don't question me. Just watch the kid." He turned and walked out the door without another word.

While her own kids were dressing, she fed the infant and he napped while she made breakfast. Unsure about what happened the previous night, she decided to make her rounds to see if anyone else knew why Rosemary's child was left in her care. When she walked into Janie's house, Janie squinted at her and cocked her head.

"Um. Did you forget to tell us something?"

"He was dropped off this morning. I was told to watch him...for a few days."

"A few days?" Janie drew out the "a" in days and her mouth hung open. "What happened over there?"

"I have no idea. I was hoping maybe one of you knew." She set the carrier on the kitchen table and fell into a chair. "I heard some yelling and a little bit of banging, but that's normal. I didn't hear anything strange."

"Well, whatever it is, it can't be that bad if he was just dropped off this morning. Someone had to take care of him over night and you and I both know, it sure as hell wasn't Maxwell." They both laughed at the absurdity.

After talking to Janie, Samantha didn't have the energy to go see anyone else. She took the baby and made the trek back home. When she got close enough to her own house, she could see Maxwell's truck, as well as Dr. Caldwell's car, in Rosemary's driveway. "Oh, that's not good," she said aloud. She assumed Rosemary had to be sedated like both Janie and Megan did. She wasn't there to witness either, but she heard stories of how each of them reacted when they found out the truth. She was surprised she didn't need to be sedated as well. It took her almost two months to leave her own house after she found out. She couldn't bring herself to face the other women. She was too embarrassed by what she had gotten herself into even though they had fallen for the same thing.

Samantha didn't know the exact time the doctor had arrived at the house, but he stayed at Rosemary's for at least three hours before she saw his car leave the driveway. Maxwell stayed in the house all day. That part was different. Whenever he had a blow up with any one of them, he always made himself scarce from their house for quite a few days, if not a full week.

It was four days before Maxwell went back to Samantha's house. He didn't apologize or thank her for taking care of the baby. He stopped by to let her know it would be a few more days.

"Is Rosemary okay?"

"Fine." Maxwell grabbed the doorknob to let himself out.

"Are you sure? I saw Dr. Caldwell's car over there a few days ago. Did she have a full mental breakdown or something?"

He turned back around fast, anger dancing in his eyes.

Samantha shrank into herself. "I... I'm sorry. It's just that... I was worried about her." Her back hit the wall and his fingertips dug into the side of her neck.

"Don't you ever question me," he spat at her. His face was engulfed in a bright red hue. "If I say she's fine, she's fine." His baritone voice echoed through the kitchen and the baby started wailing in the other room. Maxwell grunted and forced his arm forward with enough force to slam the back of her head into the wall before he released her and stormed out the door.

She doubled over, gasping for air. She didn't know what happened at the other house but whatever it was, now she knew it was bad. When she had calmed enough and got her breathing back to a normal rhythm, she picked up the baby to soothe his screaming. She bounced him and cooed quietly.

Samantha felt the need for some soothing herself. She always likes to pretend she could have a real conversation with the man that supposedly loves her. And every time she's reminded, he is the one in control.

She showered and dressed, put some make-up on to cover the redness on her neck, and set out to Allison's house. She was always the person everyone went to when they had a problem they needed to discuss. That problem always seemed to be Maxwell, but Allison was his most trusted. She was able to talk to him a bit more in depth than all the rest of them.

Allison hadn't heard from nor seen Maxwell since the night she told him about Rosemary. She was under the impression that bit of news would put her back in his good graces, but so far it didn't seem to be the case. She didn't even know where he had been staying for the past few days. He stopped at Megan's house and dropped off groceries for everyone the previous day. Megan told Allison that he seemed frazzled. She didn't risk saying anything more than "hello" and "thank you."

Allison assured Samantha she would try to talk to him in the next day or two. Noticing, but not mentioning the mark encircling Samantha's throat, she knew it would be the latter. She didn't want anyone to have to go through that, but she was certainly not willing to take the wrath for both of them. Especially since her and Maxwell weren't on the best terms.

She casually mentioned she would be willing to take care of the baby if Samantha wanted some time to herself, but she wanted no part of that.

Maxwell had asked her to watch the baby and Samantha made it clear that was exactly what she intended to do. She saw no reason to make him any angrier than he already was. She thanked Allison and made her way back home.

Allison was at a loss for what to do or say to Maxwell. She was concerned about Rosemary but not enough to put herself in harm's way. Maybe she would try to meet him at some point tomorrow, but she would have to play her cards carefully. She had already lucked out once when she slapped him, she was worried she may not be so lucky the second time. Even though it had been over a year, she was still waiting for that incident to come back to haunt her. She didn't think she was strong enough to survive it.

Two days later when she still hadn't seen Maxwell or his truck, she left her house just after dinner and made her way to each house in the neighborhood hoping to catch him somewhere. She asked everyone when the last time they saw him was and they all had close to the same answer. For some it was a little over a week and for the rest it was almost exactly a week. Seeing no other option, when she left Kathleen's house, she walked past her own home and straight to Rosemary's. She couldn't see Maxwell's truck anywhere out front, so she made her way to the back of the house to see if he had parked back there for some reason. Seeing nothing, she went around to the front again and knocked on the door. She knocked louder a second time and when she still got no response, she let herself in.

The light in the living room was on but that was it. "Rosemary," she called out. "Hellooo. It's

Allison. Are you home?" It seemed like such an odd question. She was just out and would have run into her if she had gone anywhere. She flipped more light switches on as she made her way through the house. It was empty. No Maxwell. No Rosemary. That was cause for concern. Where could she possibly have run off to? Or maybe that was the problem. Had she found a way to leave?

At that thought, her heart started thumping in her chest. There was no way. She could feel her nerves on edge, she ran out of the house leaving all the lights on. She sprinted down the road and pounded on Rebecca's door as she let herself in. Rebecca rose from the table at the sight of her and Allison felt like she was going to pass out. She didn't think she had ever run so fast in her life. She doubled over trying to catch her breath so she could tell Rebecca what all the fuss was about. Allison knew she was probably thinking the absolute worst and she felt bad that she couldn't speak to tell her not to worry too much.

She managed to squeak out "Rosemary isn't home." She held up a finger to tell Rebecca to give her a moment. Once she got her breathing under control she continued. "The only people that have seen Maxwell in the past week are Samantha and Megan. Rosemary is not home and the last time anyone saw her was the day she found out about us."

Rebecca couldn't even respond. She just stared at Allison with her mouth hanging open and her eyebrows raised. She wasn't sure she was comprehending what Allison had just told her. "Not home. Like she ran away not home or like she went out for a walk not home? Because no one would dare try to leave here. And she has a baby. She wouldn't have left him behind. Would she?"

That was something Allison hadn't considered. It had been quite a while since she had a little one of her own. If she thought she would be able to get away, would she have left a child behind knowing what Maxwell was capable of? No, she thought to herself. No, she would never be able to do that. But she had also seen what the realization had done to a few of the other women mentally and she wondered if that would be enough to make them leave a child behind. "No," Allison almost screamed. "She would never have left her baby behind. Maybe Maxwell had already brought the baby to Samantha's house when Rosemary left. Samantha also confided in me that Dr. Caldwell had been at the house the day after she found out. Maybe she really did have a mental breakdown and tried to leave after he took the baby." She pondered her own questions for a moment. "I'm going to have to talk to Samantha again to get a full timeline."

"I think that would be a good idea. Before we get all worked up, let's make sure Maxwell or the doctor didn't just take her somewhere."

Allison cocked her head. "Please tell me you haven't forgotten that other women have gone missing. This is serious, Rebecca."

She cast her eyes toward the floor and spoke quietly. "I haven't forgotten. I'm just trying to lie to myself until we know for sure what's going on. Situations like these scare me. It could happen to any one of us."

Allison left shortly after and stood at the end of the driveway debating whether to go to Samantha's now or in the morning. She decided it could wait until morning and made her way back to her own house. She was just about halfway up her driveway when she saw her porch light reflecting off a truck and she stopped in her tracks. Maxwell. She wanted to run and hide. She was not prepared to talk to him. And she was a little afraid to see him. What if someone else had told him she was asking questions about Rosemary? Knowing she didn't have much of a choice, she trudged up her driveway. Before she opened the door, she took a few deep breaths to calm her nerves and rapid heart rate.

"Hi. I didn't expect to see you today."

Maxwell was sitting on her couch. His body looked tense, but she couldn't quite figure out his facial expression. "Come sit down. We need to talk for a moment."

Allison didn't want to go anywhere near him. Knowing she didn't have a choice, she sat on the opposite end of the couch like she was a grade school student who had just gotten caught doing something wrong. Her hands were folded in her lap, her knees were pressed tightly together, and she hunched her shoulders.

"I'm guessing there's been some talk about where Rosemary's been the past week or so?" Seeing the look on her face he almost wanted to laugh but wasn't in the mood to do so. "Don't worry about it. I figured you were all asking questions at this point. I would love to put an end to all the questions and concerns about her, but I can't. What I can tell you, and I'll let you relay the message to everyone else, is that Rosemary is gone. She's gone and she will not be coming back."

Allison just stared at him with her mouth agape. What was that supposed to mean? Did he make her go away or did she run and actually manage to get away? "When you say she's not coming back? What are we supposed to do with her baby?"

"Samantha will take him."

He said it so matter of fact she assumed Samantha had no idea she had just adopted an infant and doubted she would have any say in the matter. "Okay," was the only response she could utter.

To her surprise, he stayed with her that night and left before she woke up in the morning. He didn't specify when to tell the others, so over her morning coffee she made up her mind to invite them all to dinner. Once they all got together, she would tell them. She persuaded her oldest to go around to all the houses and invite everyone. She started clearing spaces to put the fold-up tables and chairs that she dragged in from her shed. The women would eat in the kitchen as they always did, and the children would be in the living room area. It didn't give them much privacy, but the kids never had any problem carrying on a conversation among themselves.

She decided to make dinner easy on herself and threw a pot roast and vegetables in her crock pot. That would be more than enough to feed all of them, and she wouldn't have to worry about cooking anymore. She sat at her table for almost an hour trying to figure out how to break the news to everyone. She knew as soon as she spoke, they were all going to bombard her with questions, and she wouldn't have answers to any of them. Straight and to the point is what she decided on.

She finished setting out all the chairs and triple counted to make sure she had enough. She stacked plates at one end of the counter, she would fill in the middle with bowls of meat and the vegetables and she put silverware and napkins at the other end. She placed a glass at each chair and considered her physical work done for the day. The rest would be purely mental, and she was dreading the entire evening.

As people began to arrive, they let themselves in and Allison directed them straight to the kitchen to begin filling plates. She figured the sooner she got everyone settled at the tables the easier it would be to not have to ignore their questions before she got a chance to deliver her message. Her plan was to start speaking immediately after she got her plate and that's what she did.

"Okay all. I invited everyone over because I have an announcement to make. I am not happy about having to relay the message. Before I say what I need to say, I feel the need to tell you that I know you're all going to have a million questions. I do not have any answers. So, here it is. Rosemary is gone. She is not coming back."

Everyone stared at her in awe. She looked around at each of their faces, they were just blank slates. It was as if they couldn't tell if she were joking. All of a sudden, realization hit, everyone started yelling their questions at once. Allison knew it was going to happen and she almost laughed when it did. Twenty questions at once and she couldn't answer any of them. She tried raising her hand to stop them, slapped the top of the table, and finally barked "Stop," which seemed to do the trick. "Again. I know you all have questions but after what I just told you, you know just as much as I do. Maxwell stopped by last night and told me exactly what I just told you. She's gone and she's not coming back. That's it. That's the end of her story with us. It would be beneficial, I think, for all of us, to leave it at that. Don't question it anymore, don't talk about it, just leave it as it stands. It'll be just like it was before she arrived. This isn't the first time it's happened; we've gotten through it before."

Samantha raised her hand just a bit above the top of the table like a shy school aged girl. "Um. I have her baby. What am I supposed to do?"

Allison had forgotten about that part, her stomach twisted into knots. "For the meantime, keep caring for the baby. Next time you see Maxwell, ask him about it." She could see heads nodding in agreement around the table. The rest of the meal was eaten in silence while the children were happily chatting away, with no idea what was going on.

The news from dinner made Kathleen uneasy. She sat on her couch replaying what Allison had said. Whatever happened to Rosemary could have happened to her. She had thought about trying to run. She thought about how badly Maxwell had injured her on a few occasions and after what she heard earlier, she was grateful she was still there. Janie's words came flying back to her. Two years ago, she told her, "That's the part you'll struggle with the most. We don't feel like we're trapped here anymore." Tears started running down Kathleen's face. Janie was right. She didn't know whether that made her happy or sad, but she had to agree, she wasn't trapped anymore. She had a family here. A large, loving family. It was more than she had ever had.

Ten Years Later

Chapter XVIII

Over the next ten years six more woman had arrived and two of them disappeared. Thirteen more children were added to their family and only ten of them were still alive. The other three died much in the same way as Kathleen's baby, Abigail did. Allison had been removed from the group two years ago as she was caught once again telling Maxwell that someone was planning on trying to run. It wasn't because the women didn't want someone to have their freedom, it was because they felt they couldn't trust Allison.

Kathleen still spoke to her once in a while. Allison had found a route that would take her through the woods behind her house and she could come up to Kathleen's back door without being seen by anyone else. The last two years had been hard for her. She still had her children but she looked visibly worn. She was lacking the necessary human, adult interactions. She only got to see Maxwell once or twice a month and she kept her distance and only visited Kathleen every two to three months.

Kathleen had two more children now, her youngest being three years old. A few of the so called children were now adults between the ages of eighteen and twenty-four. Kathleen was having a hard time imagining that the first child she saw with Maxwell was now almost the same age she was when she met him. She was still teaching all the younger kids and every day she would go outside with them for a full hour after lunch and they would run around and play and doing that kept her feeling young.

She did find it odd that the adult aged children still never left the neighborhood unless Maxwell took one of the boys with him when he went out. None of them seemed even curious about what else may be out there. They all still lived at home with their mother and none of the women saw them as adults. The children didn't act like adults. Aside from helping with building a new house or barn or maybe snow blowing a driveway or their road, they had zero responsibilities. It was very different from what Kathleen would expect of adults but then again, they didn't live ordinary lives. They had no outside influences and they never learned how to be defiant because that just wasn't allowed here.

Kathleen did notice that Cayden was going out with Maxwell more often than not lately, and it made her wonder what they were doing. Surely Maxwell wasn't still using his son as a lure to talk to women? He was much too old for that now. She also noticed that they had started building another house much further away than the ones that were already standing. She wondered why it was being built so far away. All the women that had come in after her had their houses built between her house and Samantha's. The other side of the road still had plenty of land left to build on. This new one was further down Kathleen's street and the only one that was past her house. She had no idea how far Maxwell's land extended. Maybe it was already his or maybe he had purchased more property without her knowledge. All at once, the anger from all those years ago came flooding back to her. It wasn't something she thought of often anymore. It seemed like a lifetime ago.

At this point, Kathleen didn't care either way if Maxwell ever came home. The only thing she hoped for was that if he did, he was in a good mood. Luckily for her, she had had some good runs where he was in a good mood, at least on her nights, for two months or so. It wasn't quite as fortunate that he seemed to build up the anger during those months and it all came out at once. Over the past ten years Kathleen had suffered from broken and fractured ribs multiple times and more head trauma than was sufficient for a lifetime. She was sure every inch of her skin had seen at least one bruise and there was a scar remaining on her wrist from a particularly brutal night when Maxwell held her arm over the stove. She watched all the other women go through it but she was helpless to stop it. They never talked about it. They only supported one another when the need arose.

Early the next day, Kathleen watched Maxwell and Cayden leave in his truck from Allison's house. She took her opportunity, dressed quickly, and set off down the road. She rarely went for a walk in that direction because there had never been anything down there. She didn't even notice the house going up until two weeks ago. While she was sitting on her front step after lunch, she saw Maxwell's truck go by her house and she struck out the next day just far enough so she could see what they were doing. There was a small patch of wooded area just beyond her house that obscured her view so she had to make her way down the road a bit. She had no idea how long they had been working on it but it looked to her like a complete structure.

Today, she got closer than she had dared on any previous attempts and she could see that there were windows and a door in place now. Something caught her eye as she was looking at the house. It was far back, beyond the stretch of open land. Where the woods met the end of the yard she could see white boards shining through the trees from the early sunlight. She ran as fast as she could to the middle of the open space but couldn't tell even from this distance what they were. Not wanting to risk the men catching her when they came back, she quickly made her way back home.

After lunch she headed over to Janie's house to ask her if she had ever been down the road that far. She kept imagining the pieces of wood in her head and she was curious as to what they were. Maybe Janie would have an answer for her.

She found Janie at her kitchen table clearing the plates from lunch. "Oh, I'm so glad you're here. It feels like I haven't seen you forever." She smiled broadly.

"I just saw you at dinner last night," Kathleen laughed.

"I know. But it still feels like forever. I've been severely lacking in the 'adult conversation that doesn't include my children' thing lately. I think I really need to leave my house more."

"You can always come to my house. It may not be adult conversation but my three year old can talk to you for hours. You'll probably only understand half of what she says but it's a conversation." Both of them laughed.

"I don't understand where she gets that from. We all know that Maxwell rarely speaks and you talk but not anywhere near that much. Are you sure she's not my child?"

Kathleen grinned. "Maybe a maternity test would prove beneficial." They were both silent for a moment. Kathleen was sitting at the table drumming her fingers and Janie was making a fresh pot of coffee. "So, listen. There is a reason I stopped by today. Do you remember me telling you a few weeks ago that I thought they were building a house further up the road?" Janie was nodding her head. "Well, it's almost complete. I saw Maxwell and Cayden leave early this morning so I took a chance and ran down there to see what was happening. But when I was there, I noticed something and I thought maybe you might be able to tell me what it was." Janie turned toward her with her eyebrows creased.

"I've never been down that far. The furthest I've been is your house. We live in the middle of nowhere and I always thought that would just make it even worse to go where there were no houses."

"Oh," Kathleen sighed. "Maybe you'll know anyway?" she shrugged her shoulders. "The new house has a relatively large back yard just like all of ours but the tree line is much closer to this one. So, while I was over there spying, I spotted something in the woods. In the sunlight I could see all kinds of boards standing up behind the trees. My first thought was that it could be some kind of fence. It looked like the wood was painted. I tried to get a better view of them but when I got about halfway through the yard I got scared and ran back to my house. I didn't want to get caught, you know. Do you have any idea what they could be?"

Janie stared at her with a blank expression on her face. "So, you saw pieces of wood, in the woods, and you're wondering why?" She chuckled a little bit as she poured the coffee into their mugs.

"Not just pieces of wood. Painted pieces of wood that were standing upright in the trees. It was very weird."

Janie set the mugs on the table and sat down. "Well, honey, I have no idea what they are. But if you're curious, we'll get up early tomorrow and when the men leave, if they leave, we'll go check it out. We'll run into the woods from my backyard and take the long way through. Lesser chance of getting caught if we're not out in the open."

Kathleen smiled. "You'll really go with me? You're the best, Janie."

The next morning, both of them had the same idea. They each sat on their front porch with coffee in hand waiting to see if the men drove by. They did, and as soon as the coast was clear, Kathleen threw on her shoes and ran to Janie's house. They left through the back door and even though both of their hearts were racing at the idea of getting caught, they casually made their way back to the wood-line. Kathleen was thankful it was such a distance from the houses because twigs and leaves were cracking and crumbling under their feet and the harder they tried to be quiet, the louder their footsteps seemed to get.

Taking the long route, it was almost a fifteen minute walk before they could see the back of the new house. When the boards came into view they both stopped in their tracks. The sun was creating rows of light between the openings in the trees and seemed to settle perfectly on what Kathleen had seen the previous day. Both of their hearts were pounding and without averting their eyes they knew the same look of horror was on the other's face. In the clearing, just beyond the tree line of the backyard, fourteen white, painted crosses stood facing them. Five loomed larger than the others. The rest were only a foot high.

Janie was the third wife to arrive after Allison and Rebecca so she had been in the neighborhood to see almost everything that had happened. As she stood there staring, she began a checklist in her head, assigning a name to each of the crosses while tears welled up in her eyes. Her body began to shake and goosebumps popped out all over her skin. Tears spilled over her cheeks and she wondered which cross belonged to which woman and which belonged to each child.

Kathleen wasn't privy to any information about people who may have come before her so she just stared in wonder and confusion. When she finally turned her head she felt weak as she took in the look on Janie's face. "Are you okay?" She was in shock herself but she was concerned about Janie looking so visibly distraught.

Janie nodded her head twice. The movement was so slight Kathleen almost didn't notice. "Our babies are in there." Her voice was weak and she turned and started walking through the woods toward home.

From her viewpoint, it looked like Janie was being moved by a force other than herself and it took Kathleen a moment to process what she had said. Once she understood it, her muscles cramped up and she doubled over before releasing the contents of her stomach. *Our babies are in there.* Had Janie lost a baby as well? She glanced up at the small crosses again and her body reacted violently. She could hardly keep her balance and had to lay her hand in the leaves to steady herself.

She had no idea how long she stayed like that but she was afraid if she moved, her body would reject the idea again. She knew she needed to go check on Janie but she wanted nothing more than to curl up in her own bed and hide from the world. After almost thirteen years she was humiliated by the fact that there were still so many things that happened right in front of her and she had no idea. She never checked to see if Abigail was in the grave they dug in the backyard. Why would she ever think she wouldn't be? She wondered for a moment what the size difference in the crosses signified and the answer hit her all at once. Every time they were told someone "wasn't coming back" it meant they were buried here. Until now, there was never any reason for them to think the women were actually dead. Kathleen counted the crosses one more time and figured she must be wrong, the totals didn't add up. She would have to ask Janie later.

She stood slowly to make sure that her body would allow it and set off toward home. She decided to give it a few hours to see if Janie would come to find her first but she didn't have to wait long to find out. Janie was sitting on Kathleen's back porch with her legs hugged tightly to her chest and her cheek resting on her knees. When Kathleen got closer Janie picked her head up.

"I'm sorry I left you. I just never expected to see that. I assumed it would be something like a fire pit or maybe someone had made a make shift tent or something. I was not prepared to see a graveyard."

Kathleen sat down next to her. "How do you know our babies are there?" She knew the question was going to hurt Janie but she needed to know the truth. She wasn't aware, until that morning, that Janie had lost a child.

"I matched them up. The larger crosses belonged to the women that had moved in here and then disappeared. The smaller ones are for the children we've lost. The numbers of each match up perfectly." She put her head back down on her knees. Kathleen noticed her body was still trembling.

She reached out and rubbed the top of Janie's back. "I'm so sorry, Janie. I didn't know." They both sat in silence for a long while before Janie stood up and made her way back home.

Kathleen sat on her back step a little longer questioning everything she thought she knew about her life here. They had lost three women since she arrived which meant there were two before her time. What made the women that were still here so special? Why did they survive when others didn't? And why didn't those who knew her pain tell her, when she lost Abigail, that they had also lost a child? She was having trouble figuring out why she didn't speak up when other children passed away after her own. She was trying to make sense out of what she had seen but all she came up with were more questions with no answers.

When she awoke the next morning, she took her coffee outside and sat on her back step again. She heard a bang from next door and looked over at Janie's house. She could barely see the house itself from where she sat but after a moment she saw four women tiptoeing through Janie's back yard. She couldn't see their faces but assumed it was what she referred to as her original crew," Janie, Samantha, Megan, and

Rebecca. Janie must have made her rounds throughout the previous afternoon and was now escorting the others to see the final resting place of those that had disappeared. She couldn't help but wonder if any of them, besides Janie, also had children there.

She wanted nothing more than to cry and grieve for Abigail all over again but the tears wouldn't come. She wondered if it was because anger was now the more prominent emotion or if it's because she was relieved that Abigail wasn't alone. She'd never given much thought as to whether she believed in an afterlife or not but it was comforting to think that maybe there was someone watching over her little angel.

Since the majority of women that would have a view of both her house and Allison's were gone, Kathleen ran inside, dressed, and made her way over to Allison's. She needed to know if she knew about the graveyard and if she knew with certainty who was in it. Because people had stopped visiting with her, Kathleen thought it would be appropriate to knock on Allison's door rather than just walking in. When she opened it, she looked shocked.

"Kathleen. What are you doing here?"

Without answering, she invited herself in. "I found something the other day and I need to know if you have any information about it."

Allison just stared at her for a moment unsure of what to say. "Okay. What did you find?"

"I'm not sure if you know this or not, but Maxwell and Cayden are building a house down the road, past my house. I went for a walk to see what it was that they were doing down there. When I looked behind the new house, I found a graveyard." Allison's face went from interested to drawn and white as a sheet.

"A graveyard?" She squeaked.

"A graveyard. Complete with wooden crosses. Janie thinks it's the women who have disappeared and the children that have died here."

Allison looked like she was going to throw up. "Wait. Wait, wait, wait." She held up her hand to stop Kathleen from replying. "So you, or Janie, rather, thinks that Maxwell killed those women? Our neighbors? Our sister wives, if you will? She thinks that he killed them and buried them in a graveyard in the woods?"

Kathleen cocked her head and stared at her for a moment accusingly. "I never said it was in the woods. I said it was behind the house." She could feel nothing but rage growing inside her. Did she really read Allison so wrong for all this time?

"Uh, well. I have never seen it before so I assumed it was hidden in the woods. It would be too obvious to find if it was sitting right in the field, wouldn't it?" Her heart was pounding and she was beginning to sweat. She was silently praying the Kathleen believed her. She didn't think she could handle losing her friendship as well. She was practically a recluse as it was.

"I didn't think about it that way. But, yes, you're right. That wouldn't make any sense." She still wasn't sure if she believed her or not but she wanted to give her the benefit of the doubt. "So, you really didn't know about it?"

"Of course not. I wouldn't ever be able to keep something like that to myself. I would have had to tell at least one of you."

Kathleen squinted at her. She wanted to blurt out "telling people things is why nobody likes you anymore." She knew it would sound awful childish but she still had to bite her tongue. Despite everything, she did still like Allison. She didn't trust her as much as she once did but she still liked her. She took her leave and went to Janie's to see if she was home yet. She wasn't. Kathleen wanted to know what they had been doing out there for so long. It had been over an hour already. She just hoped they had the sense to get out of there before Maxwell came home. She was worried that if they got caught, they may end up staying there permanently.

No one said another word about the graveyard for the next six months. It was an elephant in the room but no one dared to bring it up again. At least not as far as Kathleen knew. She still thought about it and she had been back many times to visit Abigail. Even though she wasn't sure which cross was hers she was trying to make up for all the years she had unknowingly abandoned her by visiting an empty grave in her back yard.

Cayden had moved out of Allison's house and into the new house down the road. It wasn't anything that got an official announcement and neither was the fact that he brought a woman home to live in his new house. Each of them were told in turn by Maxwell and were forbidden to say anything to anyone else about it. Kathleen wondered why is was such a big deal. A few years back they had started a tradition of having a get together when Maxwell was bringing home someone new. Why should Cayden be any different?

Chapter XIX

Kathleen couldn't help but wonder what Allison was feeling at this moment. Cayden was her son and he had just brought his first wife home the same way Maxwell had once brought her here. She didn't know if it was something to be excited about, the same way it would be if they lived normal lives, or if she should be devastated to know that her son was exactly like his father. Kathleen was worried because she had a son as well. Is this what she had to look forward to in another ten years? Not knowing how she was supposed to feel about her own first daughter-in-law upset her. She didn't think she would be able to handle it. Maybe that's why they weren't allowed to discuss it.

It took two weeks before Cayden's wife, Brianna, came around to introduce herself. She looked far too skinny and ragged, like she hadn't had a haircut or a decent meal in months, but she was sweet. Kathleen didn't ask her outright how old she was, guessing no older than nineteen. It made her sad to know that Brianna was so young, and she had just made a choice that there was no coming back from.

She spent the entire day at Kathleen's house. It took every bit of control Kathleen had to not push her out the door and tell her to run. Run as fast as she could and not ever look back. But she knew that would do more harm than good. She didn't want Brianna hurt and she hoped and prayed that Cayden didn't possess Maxwell's mean streak. She calmed her own nerves by reminding herself that she never saw Maxwell raise a hand to any of the children and he never hit her in front of any of her own children.

Brianna and Cayden's house was further away from hers than Janie's was but she tried to stay positive since she hadn't heard any arguing or yelling since Brianna arrived. Throughout the day, Kathleen learned more about Brianna than she ever thought she needed to know. Yet the more she learned, the more everything made sense. She seemed to be a bit clingy and overly talkative and it seemed as though she wanted to please Kathleen with every answer she gave. Kathleen thought it was strange until she learned Brianna had been homeless. All the pieces started fitting together for her. Of course she wanted to please everyone; she wanted to be able to stay where she was. She wanted food and shelter. She probably needed someone to show they loved her.

Kathleen couldn't decide which would be worse, being homeless and alone, or being brought to a place like this with no idea of what you were getting yourself into. Cayden may have saved her, but he also dragged her into a completely different lifestyle under false pretenses. Her thoughts shifted. She wondered if Allison had been homeless as well. Did Maxwell just pick her up off the street and drag her here with promises of a great future? Maybe that would explain why she's so loyal to him. As far as Kathleen could tell, Allison was the only one of them who still loved Maxwell. The rest, including her, just tolerated him because they were forced to. He was the one that provided them with food and shelter, but they all were more loyal to each other and valued each other's company and support much more than they did his. She wondered if Maxwell knew how they felt or if he even cared that none of them loved him anymore.

Brianna was more than a little curious as to how Kathleen ran her household. She asked every question she could think of about cleaning and cooking and bedtimes for her children. Kathleen wasn't sure how to answer those questions honestly without giving away how they all lived. Every woman here had certain rules for her own children and her household, but it was a group effort between all of them. They watched each other's children, they helped to clean the other's homes. They gave advice and helpful hints and even disciplined children who weren't their own.

When Brianna asked another question about children, without thinking, Kathleen responded, "Maybe you should ask Cayden's mom." Brianna's chipper attitude diminished, she looked at the floor.

"He doesn't have one."

Kathleen thought she was going to fall over. Her eyes widened and her jaw dropped. "Oh. Do, um...do you know where she is?"

"Yeah, I guess she died in an accident or something but he was really young so it doesn't bother him much. He was raised by his dad, Maxwell. I guess he lives in one of these houses somewhere. Do you know him?" Her demeanor perked up again when she asked about him.

"Yeah... I know him."

Kathleen was uncomfortable with the conversation and she wanted to move on. "Um, maybe you should ask Allison then. All of us kind of help each other out with our children but I think Allison had a couple of years by herself with a child before anyone else moved into the neighborhood."

"Oh. That would be perfect. I'm not sure why I'm so concerned with it now anyway. I'm not expecting yet. I guess I'm just planning for the future. I'm a little out of my element here. I haven't actually had a place to take care of since I lived with my own mom years ago. I'm not sure I remember how to do all these things. And I just really want to make Cayden happy, you know?"

"I understand. But I think everything will come back to you if you just give it a little bit of time. And don't forget, we all help each other out. You won't have to do everything by yourself." She did her best to sound positive about the experience that Brianna was likely to have but in her mind, she knew it wouldn't be long before she realized what was happening. And from what Kathleen could see, she was a smart girl.

She just hoped she wouldn't do something stupid when she found out the truth.

A few days later Kathleen was enjoying a glass of iced tea on her back porch when she saw Allison running in a crouched position toward her. She was immediately concerned as Allison hadn't made her way over to her house in months. When she got close enough Kathleen stood and started walking toward her. "Are you okay?" She saw Allison raise her hand to her lips to silence her and she stepped back onto the porch.

"Let's go inside. I need to talk to you." She grabbed Kathleen's shirtsleeve and pulled her into the kitchen. "I'm okay. But I need to talk to you and I need you to listen to me. Really listen to what I'm telling you." Her breathing was labored and she sounded panicked.

"I always listen to you."

"No, I need you to listen to every word that I say. I need you to memorize the facts that I'm giving you so you can relay them when it's appropriate. Please don't ask me any questions. Just let me tell you what I need to tell you." She looked desperate and Kathleen was confused. As far as she knew, no one spoke to Allison. What kind of information could she possibly have?

"Okay. I'll listen to what you're telling me. But I don't understand what could be so important. You look really stressed." She poured Allison a glass of iced tea and motioned for her to sit down at the table.

"All right. I'm just going to dive right in and tell you everything." She took a deep breath and began. "I'm scared. I know the others haven't spoken to me in a long time and I completely understand why. I'm still not sure why you feel the need to continue talking to me but I'm glad you do. Maxwell has been acting strange lately and I think, after the way he acted towards me yesterday, he may be planning to get rid of me. Of course, he can't just go drop me off somewhere because I know way too much about him and about this whole situation."

Kathleen opened her mouth to protest but Allison shushed her. "Kathleen, I've been here for what feels like forever. I know Maxwell's life. I knew him before anyone else here. I knew his family and where he grew up. I need to tell you everything I know about him. I need you to know what I know. And I need you to promise me, promise me that you'll get away from here. Take all the information I'm giving you and tell the police, the neighbors, the news stations, tell anyone and everyone who will listen to you. Please?"

Kathleen sat there with her face scrunched up and no idea how to respond. Her heart was pounding and she was feeling anxious. Allison seemed in such a rush to relay years of information but she didn't understand why it came on so suddenly and why she was afraid of Maxwell after all these years. She had been here longer than anyone. She was the trusted one, the one he would choose to keep if he ever got to the point of only being able to have one woman left. "I promise."

"From what I've heard, Maxwell gives everyone the same story about his family when he meets them. He tells them his parents are dead and his brother died in a car accident. The part he doesn't tell them is that he was under suspicion at one point for the murder of his parents. After their death, he moved in with his grandparents. And his brother."

"I thought..."

"Shh. Let me finish. He moved in with his grandparents and his brother because his brother was still alive. He didn't die in the car accident and he wasn't driving like Maxwell tells everyone he was. Maxwell was driving. After it came out that his parents had been murdered, the police also looked into the car accident more thoroughly. They were trying to find a connection. They thought Maxwell purposely tried to kill his brother. Thankfully for him, his grandparents were very well off and they were able to find a lawyer that managed to clear his name before he faced any charges.

"Maxwell has never worked as a lawyer a day in his life. All of his money came from his grandparents' will and estate. They left everything they had to him because he was the only grandchild they had." She held up a finger again to stop Kathleen from interrupting her thought. "Yes, I know he had a brother. But the accident changed him. He suffered from massive head trauma and was never the same. Their grandparents allowed him to live there because Maxwell begged them, but they would never give him a dime. They had money and the personality to match it. If it was up to them, they would have had Maxwell's brother committed, not because he was crazy or dangerous, but because he was no longer the grandchild they knew. It's actually funny to think about because he seems perfectly fine, but they wanted to disown him because his personality changed."

"How do you know he seems fine? Did you know him before the accident?" Kathleen's eyes widened and she leaned forward to make sure she didn't miss Allison's answer.

"No. But I've met him...and so have you."

Kathleen's mouth dropped and she tried to tell Allison that she had no idea who his brother was. She was only ever told that he had died in that accident.

"Maxwell's brother, as difficult as this may be to hear and comprehend, is Dr. Caldwell. That's why he only ever allows him to help us when we need a doctor. He knows his brother isn't going to say anything to anyone. He can't. He doesn't have a job, he has no means to be able to support himself. Maxwell pays all of his bills and keeps him clothed, fed, and sheltered, just like he does with us. Without Maxwell, he has nothing. Maxwell has just as much control over him as he does all of us. And Dr. Caldwell is terrified of him. He knows exactly what Maxwell is capable of. He's seen it all first hand."

"I'm not sure I understand or believe any of this."

"Years ago, I was able to gain Maxwell's trust. It's kept me in a good position for the most part. I'm able to talk to him easier than most of the other women here and he responds much better to me than he does to anyone else. I threatened to leave a number of years back, I think there were three of us here at the time. But Maxwell kept me here by telling me about his past. I know he killed his own parents. I know that he was driving when his brother was in that accident. Dr. Caldwell even admitted to me that the story Maxwell gave me is accurate. He has killed a number of times, he will kill again. I don't believe, at this point, that I will ever make it out of here but I need you to. If I disappear, you absolutely must find a way out so you can tell people what I'm telling you. Someone needs to know. Someone needs to stop what he's doing."

"Allison, I..."

"Things are never going to get any better and he's trying to make our kids do exactly what he's doing. I don't even have a guess as to what his plan is for our girls. But I do know he wants the boys to follow in his footsteps. There is a ton of land out here that is owned by him. Even with all his sons, they would be able to keep his tradition going for probably two more generations. And the number of males in his bloodline would grow exponentially which, I think, is what he was aiming for originally. He wanted a family to call his own but he wanted a family that would abide by his rules. He loves power, he always has. Growing up, he never had any. From what he told me, his father treated his mother the same way he treats us, but his father didn't stop there. He did the same thing to Maxwell and his brother." Allison stopped for a moment to collect her thoughts and Kathleen remained silent. "The only reason his grandparents lived a normal life was because he wanted to ensure they left him all their money. He couldn't risk getting rid of them before they had a chance to change their wills and he couldn't take the chance of having the police question him again. Within a week of his grandfather passing, he already had their house sold. He auctioned off their furniture and all their belongings and cleaned out their bank accounts. Their lawyer, the one who helped Maxwell with the estate, owns the office that Maxwell claims to work for. He's the same lawyer that got Maxwell's name off the suspect list. I'm guessing Maxwell paid him off pretty well since he allows him to use their company name for personal reasons."

"Can I ask a question now?"

"Yes. But quickly. I need to get back home. If Maxwell catches me over here, he really will kill me."

"I'm still a little confused about his brother. If he went to school and got a degree, why is he depending on Maxwell to take care of him? Why didn't he just start practicing when he got out of school?"

Allison almost wanted to laugh. Poor, naïve Kathleen. "Honey, he never went to school. Everything he knows he learned from textbooks that Maxwell brought him. He doesn't have a degree, he didn't even graduate from high school." She stood and put her glass in the sink. "I really have to go." She grabbed Kathleen around the tops of both her arms, her fingertips digging into her flesh. "Promise me you'll tell someone."

Kathleen's body wilted under the pressure of what Allison was asking. "I promise you. I will."

Chapter XX

Two days later, Maxwell came storming in. The entire house shook with the force of him slamming the door behind him. "Kathleen. Where are you?" His growl, mixed with his heavy footsteps, echoed down the hallway. "Get out here."

"Stay here," she whispered to her two youngest children. "Coming," she called with the calmest voice she could muster. She left the bedroom and could see Maxwell's shadow projecting down the length of the hall. It made her feel as if his presence were everywhere. She kept her eyes cast to the floor as she made her way to him.

His hand cradled her chin and he forcibly raised her head until she was looking into his eyes. "Is there anything you'd like to share with me about the past few days?"

His breath was hot on her face and Kathleen pulled back her head as she stepped away from him. "I...I don't think so."

"Are you sure about that? There's nothing you want to share about, oh, I don't know...maybe the conversation you had with Allison while she was here?"

Maxwell matched her step for step while she continued her attempt to put some space between them. She slammed the small of her back into the edge of the kitchen counter and a whimper escaped her lips. "She only came by to say 'hi.' You know I'm the only one who still speaks to her."

"Wrong answer." His voice echoed through the kitchen causing Kathleen to flinch and a cold sweat broke out over her body. "What did she tell you while she was here?"

He annunciated each word and Kathleen watched the anger build in his eyes with each syllable he spoke. She knew she had to tell him the truth. She took a deep breath and drew her shoulders back, trying to exude a confidence she didn't feel. She blurted the words out before she lost the courage. "She told me the truth. The truth about you, about this place, everything." With the last word, she swung her arm wide, a gesture to indicate she knew it all. Her fingertip caught the edge of a juice glass resting on the counter and sent it careening to the floor. She jumped from the sharp sound of it shattering against the wood.

Maxwell seized the opportunity of her vulnerable state and shoved her into the counter, holding her in place. "Well. You do know how to be honest." His voice mellowed and a sinister smile swept across his face. "Now, you do understand I can't have two of you running around here knowing the truth. I just can't take that kind of risk. So, it looks like I have a decision to make." He released her arms and took a few steps back, "Or maybe, I'll have you make that decision."

Kathleen winced. Her eyes filled with tears, she shook her head back and forth. "I don't...I can't...please?"

"What do you think, Kathleen? Who's it going to be? You? Or her?"

Tears spilled over onto her cheeks and her muscles weakened. She knew her choice would sentence one of them to death.

"You're not going to say anything? You're not going to tell me which of you I should keep around? You don't want to beg me to stay?" His eyes never left hers and his smile was filled with amusement.

Kathleen's stomach turned. She was hesitant to answer him but managed to squeak out a response. "I don't know what you want me to say. There's no way I could ever choose between myself and Allison."

"Okay. Let's backtrack a little then, maybe it'll help you decide. Let's start with the fact that you sent Brianna to Allison's house. You really think that was a smart thing to do?"

"Maxwell, she would have made her way over there at some point, just like all the rest of us did." Kathleen heard something fall in the bedroom and she kept her fingers crossed that her children were smart enough to stay there, like she told them, even with all the yelling going on.

"Well, I can tell you Allison was thrilled to hear that she was dead. It made her day."

His sarcasm wasn't lost on her but it didn't make her feel bad like he intended it to. Instead, she felt a rush come over her and she decided she was not in the mood to get blamed for something that wasn't her fault. "I'm not the one who made up that lie. You should talk to your son. Or better yet...take responsibility for it yourself since you're so good at lying to people. Who do you think he learned it from?" Her voice was stern but she regretted every word as it came out of her mouth. She was proud of herself for saying something yet terrified about what was to come. She looked at Maxwell and noticed he was looking off to the side, nodding his head. Was he agreeing with her?

"I guess I just need to figure out which of you is more of a liability. You can't seem to keep your nose out of other people's business and Allison just wants to tell everyone the truth, starting with Brianna. You know I can't let that happen."

"Why don't you let her learn the truth? Brianna is happy here. She's happy to have a roof over her head and some food. And while we're at it, can I add that it was a really shitty thing to for Cayden to do, picking up a homeless person? But, I guess that's what made it so easy." She could kick herself. The words were pouring out of her mouth, she couldn't stop them.

Maxwell let out a laugh that sounded like pure evil escaping his body. "Pretty shitty, huh? And where exactly do you think I got Allison from, her mansion on the hill?" He began pacing the kitchen, his body more relaxed than it had been since he'd arrived. "It was really quite fun. I mean, I think I lucked out for the most part. She was as eager as could be to go away with a man who owned a house and a car. It took almost no convincing. And it didn't hurt that she cleaned up well. All I had to do was give her a couple gifts and she fell into my lap, no questions asked. It took almost no effort on my part because you don't have to break a girl who's already broken."

Kathleen couldn't believe what she just heard. She was met with an overwhelming need to protect Allison no matter what it took. She understood now why Allison was so eager to please him regardless of the outcome. After all these years, she still viewed him as her savior.

He was still pacing and Kathleen wasn't sure if he was still talking to her at this point or talking to himself. "She has become rather defiant over the past year. Sharing my secrets with you, wanting to out all of us and destroy my plans. I'm not sure I can keep her around anymore."

At once, Kathleen felt all the weight lift off her shoulders. "What are you going to do, bury her in your little cemetery, too?" She blurted the words out, unintentionally, and her hand shot up to cover her mouth. Tears stung her eyes again.

Maxwell stopped abruptly and turned to face her. "So, one of you finally found it. I'm surprised it took so long. Do the others know?" The smirk on his face terrified Kathleen more than his anger. The look in his eyes told her he had finally gained full power over the women.

She remained silent. Tears pooled at her fingers where they laid across her cheeks. She closed her eyes and nodded once, not trusting herself to speak.

"Who found it?" Maxwell was calm but his amusement seemed to wear off fast. Kathleen couldn't find the words to answer him. He glared at her for a moment and she could see the emotion change in his eyes. "Who?" he bellowed.

Kathleen jumped. "Me." She barely heard her

own voice but knew he heard her answer. Maxwell made his way toward her, his body rigid. She dared to shift her eyes away from him and spotted a knife on the drying rack. She leapt to the side as fast as she could but he was quicker than she was. When she spun around to face him, he grabbed her arm and twisted it painfully behind her.

"What, exactly, do you think you're going to do with that?" He sighed and shook his head; disappointment written across his face. "I wanted to give you the benefit of the doubt. For years I tried denying that you were as stupid as I originally thought you were. But you just keep letting me down and proving me wrong. I'm over it, Kathleen. I'm over you." He plucked the knife from her hand. "You just made your final decision."

Kathleen crumpled to the floor; her breath caught in her throat. Instinctively, she clutched her stomach and curled her body into a ball. She closed her eyes and heard the pitter-patter of tiny feet scurrying across the kitchen floor. A small hand clutched her arm.

"Mommy?"

Chapter XXI

Maxwell waited over an hour before driving to the doctor's house.

"Max? I wasn't expecting to see you this soon."

"I need your help. I messed up."

"Again?"

He nodded his head. "Bad this time."

"This time?"

"Two women...and a child."

The doctor closed his eyes and hung his head. "I'm sorry, Max. I can't help you anymore."

Author's Note

When you are finished reading, if you do not keep physical books, please consider donating your copy to your local library for their book sale or to your local prison book program.

If you, or someone you know, is a victim of domestic violence, there is help out there. **Please, do not hesitate to seek help**. Contact your local police department or local domestic violence center.

Author's Bio

Trish recently moved across the country where she found her forever home, enjoying the desert sunshine and wildlife all year long. She was born and raised in a small town in northern Connecticut. Growing up, she was always fascinated by unsolved mysteries and true crimes as well as the psychological elements behind them. As an avid reader, her go to books are thrillers, suspense, and true crime.